THROUGH THEIR EYES

RHYMES FROM THE UK

Edited By Briony Kearney

First published in Great Britain in 2024 by:

Young Writers
Remus House
Coltsfoot Drive
Peterborough
PE2 9BF
Telephone: 01733 890066
Website: www.youngwriters.co.uk

All Rights Reserved
Book Design by Ashley Janson
© Copyright Contributors 2024
Softback ISBN 978-1-83565-881-9
Printed and bound in the UK by BookPrintingUK
Website: www.bookprintinguk.com
YB0609B

FOREWORD

Since 1991, here at Young Writers we have celebrated the awesome power of creative writing, especially in young adults, where it can serve as a vital method of expressing strong (and sometimes difficult) emotions, a conduit to develop empathy, and a safe, non-judgemental place to explore one's own place in the world. With every poem we see the effort and thought that each pupil published in this book has put into their work and by creating this anthology we hope to encourage them further with the ultimate goal of sparking a life-long love of writing.

Through Their Eyes challenged young writers to open their minds and pen bold, powerful poems from the points-of-view of any person or concept they could imagine – from celebrities and politicians to animals and inanimate objects, or even just to give us a glimpse of the world as they experience it. The result is this fierce collection of poetry that by turns questions injustice, imagines the innermost thoughts of influential figures or simply has fun.

The nature of the topic means that contentious or controversial figures may have been chosen as the narrators, and as such some poems may contain views or thoughts that, although may represent those of the person being written about, by no means reflect the opinions or feelings of either the author or us here at Young Writers.

We encourage young writers to express themselves and address subjects that matter to them, which sometimes means writing about sensitive or difficult topics. If you have been affected by any issues raised in this book, details on where to find help can be found at *www.youngwriters.co.uk/contact-lines*

CONTENTS

Independent Entrants

Ryan Earl (13)	1
Alessia Wilimowski (14)	2
Medinah Ahmed (13)	6
Amanpreet Lohia (14)	9
Aisha Asad (15)	10
Alicia Kanik (17)	12
Maddy Jacques (17)	14
Imogen Wheatley (17)	17
Rameen Ali (14)	18
Isaac Jones (10)	20
Priscilla-Grace Aina (14)	22
Margaret Ambulai (14)	24
Felix Shinn (17)	26
Amelie Bremner (14)	28
Iola Kalra (12)	30
Alixander Crowther (17)	32
Oluwakayode Oluwole (15)	34
Rachel Cox (13)	37
Yumna Shaikh (15)	38
Erin Woods (12)	40
Emily Grace (15)	43
Emma Mareva (13)	44
Aimee Brown (14)	46
Sienna Kaye (11)	48
Carolina R Potje (14)	50
Ameera Aroos (18)	52
Rahee Doshi (14)	54
Ella Unwin (14)	56
Yasmin Keita (14)	58
Katelyn Williams (15)	60
Zanedine El-Naqib	62
Rosa Weitzman (17)	64
Genevieve Umahi Ndiwe (14)	66
Neil Strange (14)	68
Oscar Gray (17)	70
Oluwanifemi Tolufase (12)	72
Keisha Lehrle (16)	74
Beatrix Maspat (13)	76
Benji Marshall (15)	78
Fortune Obasi (17)	80
Joy Green (12)	82
Khudeeja Begum	84
Daniel Sokunle (15)	86
Reggie Saunders (11)	88
Aimal Waqas (12)	90
Abobaker Ahmed (15)	92
Yvetta Dixon (12)	94
Dora Bonner (12)	96
Nusaybah Bint-Khalid (13)	98
Grace Sampson (17)	100
Devon Oakes (14)	102
Amelia Longhurst (13)	104
Alyssa Muir (13)	106
Anabia Imran (12)	108
Lucy Shanks (15)	110
Asiya Akhtar (15)	112
Chinedum Allanah (15)	114
Talia Kanadil (12)	116
Teniola Ivienagbor (15)	118
Amelia Kluk (12)	119
Zachary Jones (11)	120
Ruby Ahn-Roberts (12)	121
Udochukwu Bryan Uhiara (12)	122
Ruby Howell (13)	123
Matthew Heeks (13)	124
Jayden Linton (13)	126
Farrah Bee (13)	128
Emily Kinge (14)	130
Shyann-Marie Northeast (13)	132

Name	Page
Joseph Carrothers (15)	134
Antos Thomas (14)	135
Bethany Milner (18)	136
Madeleine Fremantle (13)	138
Summer Petch (15)	139
Devon Sandell (13)	140
Tiarna Forbes (16)	142
Joshua Oyebanji	143
Chloe Ramsay (13)	144
Lucy Walton (18)	146
Rachel Moulder (11)	148
Brogan Reilly (17)	149
Kelsey Coulson (17)	150
Kai Beverton (14)	151
Fatima Hirsi (14)	152
Laura Alishat (13)	153
Mya Das (11)	154
Cynthia Guo (12)	155
Rayana Itakhunov (16)	156
Ayinza Igaga (11)	157
Farah Karim (11)	158
Huen Ting Fong (14)	159
Sofia Haacke (14)	160
Amelia Nelson (14)	162
Victoria Maleki (13)	163
Abbie Pritchard (16)	164
Harmani Dhaliwal (16)	165
Rainé Bennett-Rawlins (15)	166
Coco Blank (14)	167
Casey Clarkson (16)	168
Charlotte Easter (11)	169
Oliver Daniel (15)	170
Lucas Knibbs (13)	171
Tumi Ajibola (14)	172
Carli Zinzani (12)	174
Yasmin Ballard (11)	175
Ayooluwamide Oluwole (16)	176
Sophia Clayton (13)	178
Gaïa Renverse Harris (12)	180
Reuben McKenna (14)	181
Alice Dubroeucq (13)	182
Grace Jackson (12)	183
Adele Bagdonas (11)	184
Amaoge Okoli (16)	185
Lewis Cross (12)	186
Rustam Ofarinov (13)	187
Ewan Jones (17)	188
Sasha Green (17)	189
Hallie Whitmore-Bond (13)	190
Michelle Croll (13)	191
Ruqayyah Ajmal (14)	192
Ellinea Boiling (14)	193
Yanet Teklu (17)	194
Kamran Mughal (17)	195
Henry Duce (14)	196
Victoria Cicha (16)	197
Ava Rollinson (12)	198
Harry Scrase (12)	199
Maribel Ortiz (13)	200
Kanchan Baishkiyar (11)	201
Alisha Muchova (14)	202
Dexter Warburton (15)	203
Eleanor Pym (11)	204
Layla Williams (14)	205
Ellie Hewitt (15)	206
Harriet Eve Wingfield (14)	207
Poppy Grace Vaghela (14)	208
Sarah Gonsalves (12)	209
Alisha Marlin (13)	210
Hafsa Ahmed Bhatti (16)	211
Hashar Ahmed (15)	212
Benson Ngembus (13)	213
Callum Richard Campbell (16)	214
Olivia Rose Blake (11)	215

THE
POEMS

Apocalyptic Agony

Sometimes, I pretend the parasite doesn't grip my brain like a terrible tumour,
That my soul is free, and not locked in gloom, following other consumers.

Sometimes, I pretend I wasn't undead,
Not a consumer of inexorable dread, but with a stable head.

Sometimes, I pretend I wasn't sibilant,
That my cadaverous self was still innocent.
In the melancholy moon's embrace, I am constantly lurking,
Looking for an escape, constantly searching.

Hellfire burns within, consuming my core,
Desire, a phantom ache, relentless and raw.
In this twilight existence, I yearn for release,
My soul, a prisoner, bound by spectral chains of agony, seeking eternal peace.

My guilty conscience, a nightmare that forever looms,
In the silence, it whispers, filling the room.
A spectre of past heinous deeds, never to rest,
Echoing regrets, a relentless and unwanted guest.

Sometimes, I pretend the parasite never gripped my brain like a terrible tumour,
That my soul was free, not locked in gloom, forever following other consumers.

Ryan Earl (13)

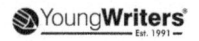

The War That Cost Me My Brother

The ear-splitting screams
The hurling of stones
The booms of bombs
And the sirens
The sound travelling through the abandoned city
All the way to our little camp
All of this
Ringing through my ear
In the middle of the night

I heard the wails of the elderly
Them knowing they would never return home
The yells of women cursing God
And the cries of men
Knowing their brothers are dead

The children
Frozen in fear
Many crying and wailing from the chaos
The little ones not knowing
True pain

I stood there
Broken inside

Only 19 but my mind was older
The horrors and the bloodshed
The images of the violence and cries of pain

It all still keeps me up at night
And the face of my attacker
The face of the monster
The monster who burned down my city
My home
My people's home
Never escapes my mind

The stench of the gas
Intoxicated into my skin
And the memories seared into my mind
The smells staining my senses
Snakes appearing in my visions
And the fires of the dead
Haunting me to this dying day

Searching through the rubble
In the morning sun
I saw those who didn't make it to camp
We left hours before night
Hoping we could make it out alive
But not all came
And not all did survive
Many died

And as the souls fled to a better place
We were left with the bodies
And the demons still flying in the skies

Seeing the face of my brother
Face down in the ground
I collapsed
And wept into my father's arms
He was only 21 but his mind was younger

He stayed back
Not willing to abandon his home
And the prosperous living his people had given him
That's what he had yelled at us when we left

He wanted to fight
But father didn't let him
Not wanting his only son to die in battle
No matter the traditions
Now seeing his face
Lying in the rubble
Dying for nothing
His life being taken without saving anyone

Years later I wished he had gone and fought
Maybe then the battlefield
Would have been safer than home

As I looked up into the bright blue sky
All I heard were screams
I heard them through the night
Through the day
Through the rescuing of my people

And I still hear them now
The yells and the pain
Absorbed forever in my broken heart
Never to be fixed
And the last words of my brother
Driving the dagger deeper
Every time I hear it echoing through my ears
And running off my tongue
You're worth nothing
But they are
They are my people
And you are not.

Alessia Wilimowski (14)

Kamakura Girl

Oh, Kamakura girl,
Is the city as perfect as you dreamt?
Is it like the wonderland you feigned?
Does the sun bid you glad tidings
And wash over Mount Fuji's summits?
Or is that too rural for you?

Oh, Kamakura girl,
Is the glutinous food of the west
Sufficient for your bland taste buds?
Perhaps yakisoba and okonomiyaki
Must be too traditional for you.
Maybe the food of stolen cultures
Is more appealing than the miso soup
That Mother made today.

Oh, Kamakura girl,
Is the coffee in the west
As quenching as Mother's tea?
Is the way she brewed the leaves
Too Japanese for you?
Can you read the whisps of cream
In your white Americano?
Just as Mother read your fortune
At the bottom of her porcelain cups?

Oh, Kamakura girl,
Are the tight and skimpy dresses
That Mother disagreed with
Better than your opulent kimonos?
Which sit forgotten in your chambers
"She will return," Mother said
Perhaps the silk is too heavy for you.
Does a white woman's attire
Suit your figure better?
Maybe 'girl' and 'woman' have no
Distinction in your mind.

Oh, Kamakura girl,
Is the bed of your comely foreigner
As comfortable as your futons?
Is the scent of his cologne
More potent than the spring sakura?
Are his lustful hands -
Which travel your unblemished body
As soft as Mother's tender strokes -
Stroking your hair as you slept?
Perhaps chastity is too cliche for you.

Oh, Kamakura girl,
Did you forget who you were
In search for the American dream?
No hair bleaching can imitate
No Monroe lipstick can distort

The forever Kamakura girl you are
In their eyes.

Oh, Kamakura girl,
Is that you perched over the windowsill?
Looking for Fuji's summits -
Which miss your gladsome visage
When all you find is a haze of lights?
Is that you?
Looking at the liberated birds -
Free from the shackles of life
Yearning to be unfettered of such?

Is that you who -
In the absence of your beloved stranger
Cries "Mother!" into the nothingness?

Mother is gone now -
You left her for the city
For 'a new life'.

As tainted as you are
You knew Mother always loved you
For the Kamakura girl you were.

You should have sent a telegram
Before her time was up -
Or maybe telegrams are too
Old-fashioned for you.

Medinah Ahmed (13)

No Opportunities

You're lucky, you know,
People don't have the opportunity that you have to grow.
You miss lessons and you think it's cool,
While others don't have the opportunity to go to school.

You put your hand up and ask for a new book,
People implore for a page, open your eyes and look.
Sexism in Afghanistan leads girls to torture,
They can't flee the country, soldiers around the border.

Pens, rulers, textbooks, you're all equipped,
Unlike your people's lives, they have a script.
Some South African children pleading,
We're lucky to be learning and our knowledge exceeding.

Sometimes, in life, we don't appreciate education,
Children from low-income countries' situation.
Together, strong change our society with determination,
There's more than one way, not just legislation.

You're lucky, you know,
People don't have the opportunity you have to grow,
Looking up at the stars, I dream of a class to belong to,
One day, I see it... my future generation's gew.

Amanpreet Lohia (14)

Wronged Child!

A short life, a tragic mishap, surely must be a mistake to take such a fool to rule.
Tick tock...
I have graves for friends, bullets for music, dirt for food.
My dignity being stolen into captivity, oh, I cried for infinity.
Humiliation is the least of my worries, out of everyone's devastation. Although, I'm sure we're all numb to that by now.
On their nourished arms held a red but abstract sticker.
The screaming set the trigger, from all their badges coated with blood-rimmed gold...
Doing as I told wouldn't save me from this, maybe?
Perhaps I await the same red and agony as the last lady...
"Spare me, I plead!" I cry and then hear a muffled sigh; nothing could come worse I thought, distraught.
Everything, including my life, is signed away in an array.
My fate is sealed but I wish for it to be peeled!
Tick tock...
My hair is tugged, my body felt like a slug, trotting away from that gassed furnace, I want to burn that place and free the forbidden race.
And the rest of us.
I am hopeless but not heartless, I am flawed but not powerless, I am just a child!
Compared to the strong, tall man I am the epitome of wrong, against him I am armed with tears, thin and unable to open a tin.

Dressed in green embodied with such a deadly symbol, he pulled me away from the camps far off the Nazi-monitored maps.
Tick tock... tick tock...
There, I was commanded to dig a hole and hide in there, like a pig.
"Shut your eyes, stay low in the hole and pray to a rock you might live, skinny child."
I cuddled a rock like a warm, fuzzy sock, my eyes were clenched shut, and I stayed put.
My eyes widened and my eyebrows flew frightened, tick tock... tick tock... tick rock!
I was wronged.
A gun danced to my forehead, swaying heavily like a hilarious pun, but dried laughter spewed from my throat, all sore and torn.
Eventually, I was shot, probably mocked, but now my ghost remains at the tourists who walk over my self-dug grave.
I was twelve, but my spirit has lasted a lifespan longer than an elf...
I was a child, a wronged one, an innocent one. But oh so wronged...

Aisha Asad (15)

Queen Penelope's Lament

My skin is melting wax, yet here I stay,
Staring down the sun of every spite spiked day;
I wait for you, Odysseus, in hope of your return,
And still, I cannot contain my sour weeps of concern.
My sternum persists to burn with an anxious grief,
Aching for your curative touch to grant me a relief.

The years pass by, weaved into the wool of my shroud,
For your dear father, Laertes, you would be so proud.
I continue to weave for years on end,
At night, I pull apart the threads, for them, I pretend;
Unravel and redo, reject those ravenous suitors,
Rabid dogs would be gentler than these uninvited looters.
Telemachus says, "They're eating me out of house and home,"
Yet he lacks your chivalry, so they'll continue to roam.

You are a hurricane of thoughts that infect my wellbeing,
A natural disaster that's natural to my nature of being.
"Penelope is patient, cunning, loyal, and worrisome,"
I work in the lab of my mind, growing my sorrows per diem:
Weeping, breaking, loving, burning,
A never-ending escape from my confinement of yearning.

I pull the curtain of my veil across my glistening cheeks,
Then walk the tightrope over the lion's den full of starving Greeks.
Troy stole you, my love, and the seas kept you hostage,

Let it take my ransom for I miss your kind heart and fair knowledge.
I am devoted to you like a moth to a flame,
A flame that burns as bright as Helios may proclaim.
Though, I must keep strong and await my prize,
I step blindly into the spotlight and perform for the watchful eyes.

Whilst paranoia and concern course thick through my veins,
My mind swims and I gasp for air, I'm drowning in my pains.
Restrained by the horizon, I stare back so serious
At the line that creates the dawn and dusk where I long for you, Odysseus.
Now I must hide and sit idly by my loom,
My age feigned and tainted by a sorrowful gloom.

I have waited 10 years for your war to be won,
Now I must wait 10 more, my war has only just begun.

Alicia Kanik (17)

Through His Eyes

Through his eyes
I could do no wrong
But that's in the past
The lyrics changed to that song

Through his eyes
He'll never love me as much as I love him
He may sit there and say so
But I can see the reality behind his grin

Through his eyes
I'll continue to make more mistakes
I'll do other things, better things
But he can't escape those heartbreaks

Through his eyes
I'm just another annoyance
A headache, a problem
His biggest disappointment

Through his eyes
There's so many better people than me
With greener eyes, browner hair
A quieter person that will let him be

Through his eyes
I won't answer the question correctly

There'll always be a better way
That he thinks of immediately

Through his eyes
I see everyone the same
Everyone's on his level
But that drives me insane

Through his eyes
I can't be saved
I won't follow the route
He's so carefully paved

Through his eyes
I'll never be what he wants
I won't reach the top step
I won't get the praised response

Through my eyes
He's loved me more than anyone else
But he's hurt me as well
More than I've ever hurt or loved myself

Through my eyes
He's everything I imagined
A knight in shining armour
Rescuing me from everything that's happened

So how do you love a person who does not love you?
Not with the same strength or intensity you do

How do you stay in a place you are not wanted?
Do you learn to get comfortable with the way they responded?

Do you sit there and wait for them to realise
That you are doing your best and want to be prioritised?
Because at the end of the day, you cannot leave
Not from a man that you're so wanting to please.

Maddy Jacques (17)

Xenization

I feel like I'm living as a stranger.
Like I'm being pushed by strong wings and pulled by tight strings.
Like I'm underwater, but there's no surface, but I don't know how to say this.
Like my mouth is covered by broken hands with loose wrists.

The words won't come when I need them, not even when life throws me new twists.
Like I'm wading through deep waters and my legs are freezing up, ready to fall down. Feeling trapped and isolated in my hometown.
Escape isn't an option.
My hope of freedom is up for new adoption.

Kids run around free, happy as can be, and then there's me.
Where's my happy? Don't I deserve that much?
I hate using other people as a crutch.
I want to cry and scream, be mad and break down.
But the most I can do is a faint frown. But oh God, I've said too much.
This is all about pain and such.

I'll be quiet now, don't pay attention to the cry of a seventeen-year-old
Who doesn't do what they are told.
My mind is yours to mould.

Imogen Wheatley (17)

The Darkest Blue

There once was a young man who stood on a bridge and rested his head, Believing he was unworthy of life and better off dead,
He had lost all hope and began to climb,
He was tired of pretending he was fine,

When a small girl did happen to appear,
As sudden as light, in his eyes so clear,
A very young girl, no older than five,
Was trying to keep him from jumping, to keep him alive,

The young man lashed out and swatted her away,
"Can't you see that I am not okay?"
He said that the girl could not possibly understand
Why he wanted to rest in the ocean's sand,

With desperate eyes, he yelled, "Just go!"
"There is no way you could ever know,
What it feels like to be hated like me"
His vision blurred and he struggled to see,

As tears streamed down his face, and he began to cry,
The young girl hugged him, told him not to die,
She told him that he was loved and that he was worthy of life,
That she would sit there until they could lessen the strife,

The young man, through his tears, told the girl to let him go,
The girl, reluctantly, agreed but it seemed there was something she wished to show,

She took the stranger and dragged him by the arm,
To a more colourful place of the bridge, seemingly more calm,

And there, to his shock, did he see
A pile of flowers, toys and a wreath,
Messages scrawled all over the ground,
You were precious and lost, now gone, nowhere to be found.

In the centre of it all, was the girl in a golden frame,
And down below, was written a name,
Marnie, may you forever lay in a peaceful sleep,
He turned, with wide eyes, to the girl who made not a peep,

But who stared into the waters and said to the man,
"I understand how you feel, I know I can,
For I stood on these railings as you did too,
And plunged deep down into the darkest blue..."

Rameen Ali (14)

Cloud

I am seen as air.
I am seen as smoke and air.
I am not solid.
I am sometimes seen as lifeless, stormy or uninteresting.
But I am much more.
More than you may see.
For you are down there and I am up here.
I see life.
I am life.
I can see you and your kind.
I see your ways. Your farms. Your foods.
Forests, cities, houses.
Deserts, mountains and valleys.
I see all things on my long-lasting journey.
I know secrets whispered in the wind.
I know myths and legends from centuries past.
I have no mind of my own, though wise I am.
I am not alone - my brethren and sistren are beside me.
There are thousands, millions of us around the world,
But some I may only meet once.
We are protectors; we gaze upon you either night or day.
We do not rest.
Shielding you from the sun's bright, burning blaze.
We are your guardians. Protectors.
Although we cannot do much, and we are very sorry for that.

If we are sorrowful, we may cry down rain, maybe scream out thunder.
If we are perplexed, it may hail.
If we are proud of you (which we always are) it may snow - to give you fun.
In the fog, we are drifting down to murmur, 'Hello'.
Now, I am deeply sorry to those who experience drought.
We're not angry at you and we know you need rain,
But we must follow the path where the wind takes us.
I know it doesn't make sense but even I cannot control nature.
We are all unique. Just like you.
We come in all shapes and sizes.
All with our own knowledge.
But we all know one thing...
As God's creation, we couldn't have asked for a better job than this.
There is so much more I wish to tell you, but I must now go.
But if we someday meet - either on mountain, or in the fog -
Or if we never meet at all, remember this...
We are seen as air.
We are seen as smoke and air.
But we are much more.

Isaac Jones (10)

Collide

My heart's pounding
Face sweating
Thoughts as loud as lightning
My senses suddenly switch off
And suddenly, my surroundings become nothing but a muffled and distant memory
My heart starts to wail, but my face shows nothing but
Pain and fury as the betrayal suddenly hits me
And like a gap in a window, my thoughts seek their chance and make
Their grand entrance
Saying
"Naive girl,
How could you think they were different?"
Was it the hug that made you feel as if you were hugging a marshmallow?
Was it the smile that could replace the stars?
Or was it
The hand that reached out to you in the fog when no one else could?
Or at last
Was it the smile that they'd shine to you under a fake impression?
Was it the jokes that were only made when their friends were around?
Or was it the tic-tac-toe games that would mess with your brain?

And then at last
The final straw came
The day you walked into the room and the rumours and whispers began
And you looked around and the muffling began
And everyone gave you a look
A look of unbelonging, a look that showed nothing but pure hatred
And now you were the distant memory that no one remembered
And you remember one thing
The hand in the fog
And you look around and the same hand that took you out of the fog
Pushed you into it
And you see their malicious eyes glimmer like the sun
And you feel a throbbing pain in your back
And you place your hand behind your back
To find the very knife that stabbed you in the back
And you want to do something but all you can do is cry
And say they told you so
So you put the key in your heart and lock it far away for no one to see
And realise
It's time to listen to your brain
Your heart is nothing but a distant memory.

Priscilla-Grace Aina (14)

Daughter, Brother, Mother

What's it like? Behind the closed door?
Can you hear my roars? Can you hear my calls?
She closes the doors, Brother's in the corner, Mother's still at work.
The fridge is empty, their courage is dull.
Help him with the homework, use your skull.
Wash the dishes, it's tradition.
You're a girl, wear your pearls and pass me the jalebi swirls.

I'm your daughter, we share the same colour and you are my mother.

Brother's at the table with an empty plate, I'm still in my room contemplating my fate.
I wear my hair up, down and straight but no matter how I wear it, you would still hate.
Your emotions turn into explosions but you tell me it's a good omen?
You're a girl, wear your pearls and pass me the jalebi swirls.

I'm your daughter, we share the same colour and you are my mother.

I brush his hair, I overwork while you're still at work.
I make his breakfast, lunch and dinner while you claim I'm only a beginner.
His homework, fold his clothes, and tuck him in but to you, I'm just a punk.

You're a girl, wear your pearls and pass me the jalebi swirls.

I grew up being a mother, I grew up without one too.
If you want to know what sucked the most, it was not having access to you.

The older child, the immigrant sibling, nothing about me is thrilling.
Reading paperwork, sorting bills were only a few of my older sibling skills.

I told myself that things would change, knowing that I was just drained.
It's been several years and the only thing I can remember is...

You're a girl, wear your pearls and pass me the jalebi swirls.

I was your daughter, we saw the same colour but clearly, you were not my mother.

Margaret Ambulai (14)

What A Wonderful Woman

I think the tale of Jekyll and Hyde is really quite fascinating.
We see this man, so lost, always oscillating
Between Good and Evil, and
That which is to society acceptable.

He has a name, a face, an identity,
A mask he wears to keep up pleasantry
But wants and needs dig deeper 'neath
The blackened leather of his sheath

Which mars the blade he tucks within
So perfect, should he let it gleam
And catch the light in splendid glee
And shine for all the world to see.

Yet for the words of other men, he hides
And to his inner wants, he chides
You are so wicked and so cruel
The sickening thoughts of an insipid fool

You are to me, the deepest depths
Of man's subconscious pained regrets
Desires of an evil man
So cowardly, a blackened plan.

For those deep thoughts that he neglects
They come to be in manifest

Such darkened ways, they pull his strings
And do to him unholy things.

But such is the hubris of mankind
To curse the makings of their mind
To listen to society's demands
And snuff their flames with shaking hands.

For had Good Jekyll looked again
To the mirror with a tarnished grin
He may have seen within his face
A better way to view his grace

I think of this now, standing here
Caked in terror, bathed in fear
Of the world beyond and all its hate
Which in this room cannot negate

The callings of a haunted soul
To shed a vessel, be reborn
To throw the mask of man away
And as a woman, greet the day.

For sad and haunted as Jekyll may have been
Hyde might have been a beautiful thing.

Felix Shinn (17)

I Know How It Feels

"I know how it feels."
It hits me like a deer in headlights
When I see what I have achieved
I'm not sure I really wanted this

I look down to my very own two hands
I look at the blurriness hazing my vision
Through tiny drops of melancholy rain

Spouting from my eyes, it seems
I put myself in the shoes of those I have hurt
Along the years, and those I still torment

The people I once loved and cared for
All flash before my eyes. I realise I have
Lost them forever

I've lost my sense of knowingness
For who I am or what I stand for
Or if I can even call myself human

Like a broken lightbulb
I flick through different people
Those I see and I myself

I realise the problem isn't
Someone else's. Someone's words
Or actions or deeds

But purely my own

I see now in different light
The person I most truly wish
I had never met

The one that torments me
Although I learned so much
From broken hands

They may struggle now too
But that is no excuse for the
Struggles they put upon me

They only feel guilty when they realise
They were the one who could change things
Who could stop treating me this way

I know how it feels to be there
How it feels to be treated in such a way that
It feels daunting to be alive

I know how it feels to have
Every tear sucked away from me
As if it belonged to someone else

I know how it feels to be so 'weird'
Everyone gave a wide berth

I know how it feels to be different.

Amelie Bremner (14)

Broken Beyond Repair

I see you frown at yourself,
As the new seeds of destruction bloom,
Squinting at your reflection,
Begging for perfection.
Wonder why you can't have a slimmer shape,
Instead, you unwittingly fill yourself with pernicious hate.
You want to have a skin as clear as smooth glass,
So why destroy it with your self-inflicted wrath?
You're falling apart in front of me.

I see you frown at yourself,
As droplets of sweat and tears maul your hopes,
Mindlessly scrolling through your toxic feed,
I see you slowly bleed.
Those manufactured women are not what they seem,
That isn't what you want to be.
You're tearing apart in front of me.

I see you frown at yourself,
As the evergreen leaves wither and crumple,
There's someone beside you,
The reality you wished to be true,
It claws and tears at your face,
Viciously altering it to the 'perfect' taste.
You're breaking apart in front of me.

I see us glare at ourselves,
The cold seeps through our bones, our heart, our soul,
Is that tormentous rupture in our frame going to be the bitter farewell?

And our sweet welcome to hell?
You didn't even know if you wanted to be me,
Are you afraid of what we'll see?
You're cracking apart beside me.

I see you grin at yourself,
As seeds of healing bloom,
Run your fingers through your freshly-styled hair,
Your face full of vibrant life,
I drink it up, draining it of joy,
Staining it with hate.
You shatter,
Cracks mar your broken, bruised face.
Broken beyond repair.

Iola Kalra (12)

The Unremitting Human Conscience

R estriction, routine, repeat.
E asing through nature's emulation,
P assion frail, individuality a bygone of time.
E asy, controlled, comfortable ignorance simple to manipulate,
A ncient ancestry stolen, now dormant, hushed like a crime.
T reasured, romanticised, suffocating salvation.

R estriction, routine, repeat.
E ach holding another, keeping each budding life alive.
P ulsing hearts grouped, living, hoping.
E arly dreams gripping, fraying, trying to soar, to fly.
A child's singular heart, repressed, slowing.
T reasured, aware, mature.

R estriction, routine, repeat.
E ast, south, north, west, interlinked, intertwined, stars to guide.
P eople below, longing for the flight.
E nigmatic, analysed creatures of the endless blue-painted skies.
A sought dream, high out of reach.
T reasured, destructive, unaware.

Their intertwined dreams, woven by my own laboured hands,
Taking in hopeful souls, escaping the reality of the dark destruction.

Dreams sewn into every being healed by her, the mother.
I recommend all designed by her nurturing hands,
Their nature, their reality, becoming mine to intimately manipulate.
Tight grips of desperation, shattering to desolation.
Misled scars slowly covered in a newly woven cold blanket.
Threads old and new, finding solace in the abyss of the mind's eye, mine to deceive.
The false reality of their shared desires, granted, replayed, forgotten. Taken.
Restricted individuality, shared.
Routinely resurfacing, haunting comfort.
Repeated at every closure of a seeking eye.

Alixander Crowther (17)

The Orange Ball

I am passed between clammy hands
Big ones, wide palms
Rough calloused ones
Hands big and small

I am passed through screens
Through photos and black and white TV,
To fuzzy and high resolution HD
Transcending evolution,
Transcending time

I'm used to the fame.
To the flashing cameras,
The goggling eyes watching my every move
My location being noted by noisy commentators

It's tiring sometimes
I get flattened out
Believe me, it's hard work
But I digress.

With the weight of a nation
Etched into my stripes
A heartbreak at one's fingertips
It all comes down to a pass
A shot
A miss.

To pass the mantle
To pass the rock
To pass the dime
For generations
And generations to come

To the children gathered in front of the television,
To those that seek the glory
To those who have reached the top
To those who wish to tread where no one has trodden before

I am poetry,
An expression,
A myth,
A legend

A ghost writer for those who wield me.

Each dribble
Each bounce
Each pass
Each shot
Another step forward.

Another legacy in the books

Passing on a vision
Passing for the future
To win the beautiful game

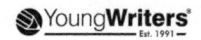

So all in all, folks

It starts with me.

The Orange Ball,
With black looping stripes,
At the dark corner of the gym hall.

What are you waiting for?

Oluwakayode Oluwole (15)

My Cat's Life

The sun is rising in the east, the grass is wet with dew.
I yearn to be outside again, I am desperate for the loo!

At last, the door is opened and I rush to get outside.
I see the shrubs ahead of me, the perfect place to hide.

Here I watch what's going on and smell the scents hanging in the air.
I can just make out who's travelled by, first squirrel, mouse, then hare.

So now for some daily exercise, I'd better chase a bird.
"He needs to keep his body sleek," those are the words I heard.

After chasing comes lazy lounging, we all know it's what we do best.
My person keeps on telling me that all I do is rest!

But what they don't know is we are always watching and listening for sounds.
If there's any tremble or rumble, my paws are instantly on the ground.

I have an extremely contented life, I do exactly as I please.
The job of being top cat is really quite a breeze.

Rachel Cox (13)

The Fall And The Rise

Drunk on ecstasy, joy is overriding my heart
As we glide through cool, cloudless skies
Oh, Father, I always knew you were smart
But this is beyond a dream in my eyes.

This is somehow better than anything
Soaring through an endless aero sheet
It's optimum, this sickly giddy feeling
And I decide this is mortal's worthiest feat.

Rising up into the eagle's level is ethereal
But, Father, I crave for more altitude;
I want, like the birds, to be forever aerial
And I'm sure the wax has by now been glued.

The sea is way below us; I can barely hear its sough
The sun never hurt the birds; so what could break me now?

My eyes crinkle into a smile as I reach for the stars
Father, I can barely make out your thin, weary frame
As the ground drifts away; by now, you seem so far -
Whilst the sun is as close to me as a candle to its flame

Its fiery heat blazes, my smile blurs with my sight
The adrenaline drowns away, leaving remorse in its wake
The wind is ripping away my wings and my flight
And as the glue melts off I realise our *stultus* mistake

As I fall from the stars' forbidden territory above
The thin line between dreams and nightmares is crossed
I look up to the sky and watch the graceful flight of a dove
Father, why must I die? Why should I fall whilst it stays aloft?

In my last moments, anticipation makes me regret our hope of it all -
How painfully ironic that the higher the rise, the harder the fall.

Yumna Shaikh (15)

In The Serene Onyx Night

Moving through the serene onyx night,
Wind stroking my cheeks,
I breathe in the crisp cold air,
And hear the sound of the creatures,
Moving through the serene onyx night.

Trees whisper after me,
In my wake,
For I am the ruler of the night,
My fierce eyes scour the land,
Glancing at the changing of scene,
In the serene onyx night.

Stars shine down upon me,
Woven into the navy heaven,
The rays of the moon,
Casting their light,
Onto the silence
Of the serene onyx night.

Silver grass sways in the wind,
The cry of the owls
Pierces the atmosphere,
The sound dancing onto my ear,
And I shriek into the muteness of
The serene onyx sky.

Because in the darkness
I can be
Whatever I want,
Free from the shackles
Of what humanity expects of me
Beneath the cloak of
The serene onyx sky.

But squinting into the blackness,
I can see
A speck of sunlight
Emerging from the horizon,
Cutting through the
Serene onyx night.

Light floods the earth,
Blinding, flashing,
I silently scream inside my head,
I don't want it to be over,
Not just yet,
I don't want to shroud myself anymore.

I can be me in the
Serene onyx night,
But then the sun will come,
And the light will throttle me,
I will slowly transform
Into what I am forced to pretend to be,

And I will hide myself
In the deathly azure day.

Erin Woods (12)

Insecurity

The monsters beneath the bed turned to what the scales read
They shed from cavernous echoes to hisses in my mind
Your words and whispers are an ode to the graves you own
Which bury the sagging skin and bone young women will soon find

They attempt to dethrone the seats of power, who relax in might
Paying homage to those who bask in accepted gold
While they thrash in fictions of fire, writhing in the night
Fighting for their place and perfect kiss, searching until old

For bliss and paradise, weightless of sin
But with weight of age, fuelled by rage
Of those untouched, scarless from their easy win
With their cursed minds and indolent ways

Whilst those in blood-soaked gowns escape from rubbled towns
And exclaim, "Hark, how the angels sing!" in a false victory
But their dreams of freedom crush beneath the heel of sneering glory
And instead, their fight is forced back by those who won't repent.

Emily Grace (15)

The Fight For Montanum

Montanum, land of the greenest field,
So peaceful it requires no shield,
"Just like those before them, they are unjust,
blessed with powers they don't deserve
that they will use to take over our sacred country,
we must stop them, no matter how bloody
the fight for Montanum gets.
Through their eyes,
Magik people are superior,
and we are inferior,"
Theon, the Ordinarie king roared,
to the applause and raising of his divine sword.
"For Montanum! For Montanum!"
half the nation cried
as his assistant handed him his sword
and he went to the Hill of Collis
to plan his ambush on the Magik people.
But it seemed he would be the one getting ambushed.
When the Magik queen stood at the top of the hill,
"I heard of your plan, your plan to kill,
from our cook as she was a spy,
you may know her, her name is Mai."
King Theon's eyes widened in shock,
but alas, no time to dwell,
a battle will soon propel.

He drew his sword,
its blade ethereal like its golden guard.
As Queen Rhonda drew hers too,
they swung their swords until their arms were numb,
and blood poured over the grass until it turned maroon.
Finally, Queen Rhonda won after hours of fighting,
and lots of dying,
from civilians who got involved,
in The Fight for Montanum.
"Through your eyes, I'm unjust and cruel,
but I am nothing more than a fool,
to cause a war from just a duel."

Emma Mareva (13)

Why Does No One Want Me?

Why does no one want me?
I lay, the only piece of fruit in the bowl, a lonesome apple
Battered and bruised from their carelessness
They had made me this way, now why was I not wanted?

I watched as the other apples were plucked from the porcelain bowl
I saw the reaper robbing me of my company grimace at my appearance
I should have known I would never get chosen
Destined for the bin or the compost heap

I should be grateful that a worm is not eating me alive
And instead, I am sitting alone in this rounded pit, watching the disfigurement darken
Gazing up at sorrowful faces filled with disgust that I am the last left
I lay in wait of death as fungus overwhelmed me, cementing me to the bowl

A few days later, my body caved in, becoming a lump of distortion
I was in so much pain, why didn't they just accept me for my wounded body?
Why was I being neglected? They had made me this way
My skin grew wrinkled as the mould scaled upwards, smothering me

I watched through the vines of mould enshrouding my eyes
At the repulsed faces as I was aggressively eased off of the china
Choruses of disgusted snorts sounded as my decomposing skin tore off
The hard, cold, metal spatula flicked me into the empty black void, ready for landfill

Yet as I was slowly dying, I glanced around
The eaten corpses of my friends littered the bottom of the bag
We all had suffered the same fate, I thought
As I let death take me.

Aimee Brown (14)

What Is Red?

I'm seen as the colour of anger, of hurt
I'm seen as a warning, a danger alert
I am an angry bull in a fight
I am the blood after a bite
I am the rage of a vicious black bear
I'm seen as an argument, a voice with no care
I am the sky when it rages and roars
I'm seen as the fury, the aggression in wars
I am the destructive flames of fire
I am the colour of an evil desire
I'm seen as the colour for conflict and fear
The cautions, the madness when the devil comes near
I am the colour of embarrassment inside
But no one ever sees my true other side
I'm not always just violence or madness
Not just fierceness or forever sadness
I am a symbol of love with a beating heart
I am the colour of relationships waiting to start
I'm not just temper or cries and screams
I am a heart filled with hope and dreams

I am bright, I am bold, there's another part to me
Another part everyone chooses not to see
I can be joyful, and gorgeous, look at me now
My beauty erupting, me showing you how
To look at me differently, to see my good side

I am love, I am sunsets, I am ambition and pride
I'm not seen as what I truly could be
I'm that feeling inside that you fail to see
I am those special warm hugs on a cold winter's day
I can make those bad feelings go away
I can be a ruby that twinkles in light
I am a beacon that glows very bright!

Sienna Kaye (11)

Behind The Mirror

You'll never be slim enough.
No, no, you'll never be pretty enough either.

Never tall enough, never short enough, never thin enough, never fat enough, never fine enough, exotic enough, odd enough, and never perfect enough.

I promise.

I promise that no matter how long you stare at yourself in that mirror, I will always, always, find your imperfections.
I'll let them haunt you in the broad daylight.
I'll let them whisper softly in your ear, reminding you that they still exist, even after you've covered them up.
I'll let them hover above your head; ever taunting, ever pestering.
I'll let them crawl into the back of your mind; always gripping your attention.
You call it insecurity.
I call it self-sabotage.

And then, it goes my way.

It's funny how a person changes so, so drastically.
I'll watch you let yourself in; lock yourself into The Hall of Mirrors.
I'll watch you pound the mirrors with all of your might.
Crack the mirror one blow at a time.
I'll watch you crumble under your own two eyes.

All you ever wanted was perfection.

Your own critical eye can destroy you; shatter you to bits; dismantle you from the outside.
Even before you've broken your first mirror, you have already lived your cursed seven years.

They call it self-hatred, but I personally disagree with that.
I call it self-obsession.

Carolina R Potje (14)

Colour Is 'Black'

From the viewpoint of Tom Robinson in To Kill a Mockingbird

In the court
Can't say a word
Don't know what the law's for
They say I raped a girl

My colour is everything
Makes it all clear
"He used this girl, made her a victim"
And the rapist stands right here

My lawyer is trying
He reveals all my flaws
But the jury is adamant
And they say I'm the cause

My life is all ruined
My daughter's alone
They don't have any mercy
This world is brutal and cold

There is no point to this
Not anymore
In their eyes, I'm a rapist
A lot less, nothing more

My colour is everything
Makes it all clear
The silence is deafening
And the words turn to fear

My colour is everything
Makes it all clear
They won't remember me in history
Because to them, I was never here

The jury is out
I'm guilty, no surprise
Even if I'd opened my mouth
I'd still be dirt in their eyes

It's not fair or right
The way this world works
Base everything on sight
And the innocent gets hurt

I hope there is a change
For them to fix the wrong
Take back all of their mistakes
And do things right for all those young

Even before I came
I knew the truth was clear
They were never going to listen
And I was going to die here.

Ameera Aroos (18)

Her Sort Of Pretty

She's pretty,
I know that.
She's smart too.
And popular.
Not the mean popular, the nice popular everyone likes.
Her parents are nice,
I've met them.
I'm over at her house so often, her dog thinks I live there.
But she's not just pretty -
She's the sort of pretty that makes you stare.
Guys like her,
When we're out, they ask for her number,
People watch as she passes,
They all want to be her friend.
They love her clothes,
They love her hair,
They love her eyes,
They love her.
Without even knowing her.
Yet, I'm sure if they ever spoke, they would only love her more.
I know I'm pretty too,
I know I'm not stupid,
I know my parents don't suck,
And I know people like me,
But it's just not the same.

I'm the sort of pretty you need to get to know.
The sort of pretty - with a pretty personality.
As a whole, I'm pretty -
As a half, I'm average
But is it so horrible
To want to be her sort of pretty?
The sort of face you fall for?
Not because I'm funny
Or nice
Or loyal
Not personality pretty.
Pretty pretty.
Pulls the guys pretty -
Popular pretty -
Pretty privilege pretty -
She's perfect pretty.
Is it so horrible
That I want to be her?
Her perfect sort of pretty.

Rahee Doshi (14)

Through Their Eyes

Our families cried, wished goodbye, crossed their hearts
That the men won't die
Feel fear, won't go near a land where no man owns.

Some comrades who given up, hope, ponder, wonder
When artillery will hit them, kill them
Why would we fight?
Not only the Germans, but the cold and the dangerous nature?
We persevered anyway.

The cold freezing eyelids together, seizing hands frozen
Making them the colours of a cold summer's breeze
Purple, red, blue, like the sky used to be
Grey pollutes the air heavily
Meanwhile, we choke on gas so thick
We could chew and unfortunately swallow it.

Lungs on fire.
We slowly decline and our collapsing lungs
Our brains shutting down, forgetting how to load
And fire our guns
Eyes slowly shutting from hypothermia and exhaustion.
All night, listening out
No sounds from our rivals
This was too concerning to ignore

Insomnia hits us like artillery shells
The damage is irreversible.

Remember when a poppy glows red
Like the blood we shed
Poppy petals ripped off one by one
Remember us when 11:11 strikes again
Now as we look down, we hear prayers
Voices so familiar, our descendants, warm-heartedly
Speaking every November
"Thanks for dying for us
And making sure your name gets
Carved on stone."

Ella Unwin (14)

This Or That?

Choose a shirt to wear today.
Seems easy - right?
Well, that's before they're in your sight,
And your unsuspecting eyes flood with fright.
Black or white or orange and blue?
Why this is suddenly scary? I have no clue.

I've been doing this for years!
How come I don't know what to do?
I only have half an hour, and it's 7:22.
A shirt or a skirt?
Or maybe just a blouse?
Whatever I pick, I need to get out of this house!

Time's running out!
I don't know what to wear.
I've only just realised, I haven't done my hair!
10 minutes, then 5.
My shoes aren't even on.
Then my alarm rings and everything just... stops.

I take a deep breath and count to 3.
Then I sit down, hands on my knees.
I pace down the stairs, past my brother, and in the kitchen, I find my mother.
She asks me, "What's wrong?"
I tell the half-truth, although I find it being uncouth.

She asks for my favourite colour.
I told her it was blue.
We continued to my room, as we both knew this was true.
She picked up a blue shirt and a black skirt.
We went to school by car, and I counted some birds.

I'm glad I asked for help, or I would've been there forever.
You should also ask for help when you're a bit under the weather.

Yasmin Keita (14)

A Day As My Dog

Look through the eye,
Tell me what you see.
It's morning, great, because I really need a wee.
I go outside, do my thing,
If I see a cat, I chase it,
Because it's my garden and I'm the king.
I am as old as can be and may only have one eye,
But people are still scared of me, even the birds that can fly.
I go back in the house and wait,
They gave me biscuits and treats, which I ate.
But there's one more thing that I love more than anything,
A bowl full of water and I drink the whole thing.
After that, I go lie down and have a sleep,
It takes me seconds without having to count sheep.
Someone wakes me up with a knock on the door,
I get up to bark, bark, bark, and bark some more.
When they're gone everything's okay,
I can go back to sleep knowing I saved the day.

Look through the eye,
Tell me what you see.
It's afternoon, great, because I'm ready for my tea.
I run to my bowls, sit and wait,
I wag my tail as they give me more biscuits and treats. Yay!
When I've finished my tea, I know what's coming,
A lovely bowl full of water. Thanks, Mummy!

I get let out and chase birds this time,
Because if I don't, it will be a crime.
After that, I'm worn out,
They won't be coming back without a doubt.
Time to go sleep and dream about everything I scared away,
For I hope you enjoyed being me for a day.

Katelyn Williams (15)

Side By Side

Clashes of glasses and sips of mighty cheers,
Happiest of nights and the funkiest of people.
The shy, forced-open, immorally joyful mouth of rum and beer,
Is a consumer of many peers.

It's a sputtering side of the road for the happily burning mouths,
Of people who shout, laugh and have lost their consciousness temporarily.
Of the people who have times of fun until those times end.
Of the people who tumble recklessly with jubilation out of the Ploughs.

The invisible line of division that burns in agony,
Through the contrast of emotions, beliefs, and lifestyles is obvious to the human eye.
The people on each side are in difference with mentality.

Across the concrete line in which cars come and go at any time,
Is a big structure that shone and still shines bright with its ever-warm, sociable smile.

It's a peaceful side of the road for the mouths that are moist with kindness.
These are the people who are content, amiable and have firm, strong minds; hearts and souls.
When they walk, they walk with keenness.

If you dare to stand between the two sides, then you are conflicted with your being.
The heart is nothing but an ornamental gift that should be kept clean.
For the one who steps foot on the road, he should be concerned with which side he is seeing.

Zanedine El-Naqib

For Sale: Baby Shoes, Never Worn

I sit still, waiting, frozen and patient.
My seams tightly sewn, my insides lined with fur,
A pink bow adorns my head, a beamish child's dream.
They look at me then leave, their eyes shimmering, their voices quiver.
What have I done wrong?
How did I hurt them so?
Designed to bring warmth, bring laughter and glee,
Destined to be worn, to be dirtied, to be tossed.
I sit still, waiting, frozen and patient.

They scream and curse, hurling accusations of who lost more.
One should have worked harder, the other should have worked less.
They glance towards me and sigh.
Pain poisons their breath, their eyes, their hands.
Their suffering fluctuates between vicious spats and icy silence.
What did they do?
What did they lose?
I lie still, forgotten, my hopes dwindling as another futile day passes.

A day rises anew, I lie desolate and alone.
Never to feel precious, never to be used.
A shift in my centre of gravity, a shift in my existence.
I have been acknowledged.

Bargaining, questioning, desperation, they endeavour to rid themselves of me.
Was I not enough?
What more could I do?
I am passed on to the next. They are released, never to look back.
I was there sitting still, waiting, frozen and patient.
But I was never worn.

Rosa Weitzman (17)

Eyes Of Wonder

In eyes of wonder, worlds unfold,
A universe within them lies,
Where galaxies of dreams reside,
And mysteries of shadows hide.

Through their eyes, we glimpse the dawn,
Where hopes are born and shadows gone,
The spark of joy, the hint of pain,
A silent story in each frame.

In their eyes, the stars align,
A costume dance, a grand design,
Each twinkle tells of distant skies,
The colours of a sunset bloom.

With every glance, a spark ignites,
With pure delight, a symphony of
Sight and sound, in eyes that see
A child grow, the beauty, joy and
Silent law.

Through their eyes, the heart exposed,
A secret garden, petals closed.
With every look comes with every stare,
We touch our souls, laid gently bare.

Through teardrops prisms, rainbows arc,
Where dreams overtake the dark,

A canvas vast of purest light,
In wonderful eyes the soul takes flight.

In every gaze, the seasons turn, and lessons
Are learned. The past and future interline,
Cause sweet and divine moments to be
Captured.

Through their eyes, we find the truth,
The wisdom found in tender youth.
A mirror to our hidden fears,
A source of light passing through our years.

Our eyes awake, the world is new,
A canvas rich with vibrant hues.
In every glance comes with heart -
Shaped eyes that see the world differently.

Genevieve Umahi Ndiwe (14)

The Football Warrior

As I walked like a lion, ready to catch my prey,
The crowd was like a music festival at night, blasting us with their spray.
Cheering us on and on, I felt my heart was like a never-ending roller coaster, which kept on accelerating,
As I stood ready for the most important match of my life, awaiting.

Boom, bash, bang, he did it again, a goal!
I punched the air in happiness as I strolled to the subs bench as the whistle went off like a rocket powered by coal.
As I sucked a tangy, juicy, and sugary orange like a superhero getting his powers.
I listened to the coach changing the tactics for our next encounter.
I said to myself, "We are going to win!" For I was filled with strength and passion.

All eyes were glued to us, it was game on!
I was on another planet just for a second - Oh no! *Boom, bash, bang*, a goal!
My teammates were looking dull, I hung my name in shame.
"My aim is to win not to lose," I said to myself angrily.

I ran and chased like the wind, determined to get glory.
The story was just starting - penalty!
This is my golden opportunity, is this going to be defeat or victory?

He shoots and he scores! *Boom, bash, bang,* goal!
We all make mistakes, but we should never give up, no matter what.

Neil Strange (14)

We Stepped

In that quiet hush of ordinary days,
where mundane minutes murmur softly by,
a moment arrives, a tapestry unravels,
life pivots on an axis unseen.

Not in thunderous crashes or flashing lights,
but a subtle shift stirred a tremor of souls,
a ripple across still surfaces of existence,
we stumbled upon a crossroads.

In the glow of city lights and in the shadows of trees,
we met that turning point, unexpected,
a whisper on fair winds and a murmur in our hearts,
an invitation to dance with destiny.

Our humdrum rhythm fractured as we embraced life unfamiliar,
our hands clasping thin threads of change,
we waltzed to a tune unknown.

It wasn't grand, this awakening,
more like some quiet unfurling of petals,
an opening of eyes long closed, and vast universe whispered secrets.

And so, beneath that broad canvas of sky,
we shed old skins of yesterday,
rustling leaves surrendering to an autumn breeze,
we embraced that shedding, brave letting go.

With hearts alight, and souls unburdened,
we marched towards far horizon,
a dawn of each new chapter, unwritten,
a saga unfolding in footsteps left behind.

Gleaming with promise, bright sun ascended,
casting shadows that danced with hope,
and so, we stepped into the dawn forever changed,
a metamorphosis complete, an evolution begun.

Oscar Gray (17)

I Am Free

I am free
Locked. Abused. Silent.
The scars under my sleeves
Are dying to be free
How I long for a voice
But I never get a choice

Taking matters into my own hands
I will escape
I will be the one to take a stand
All my memories and dreams chase me

But I am tired of crying
I am tired of getting hurt
I am tired of not having a voice
This is it
I either go or stay
And I will go

A part of me longs to go back
But no, I can't
What if this...
What if that...
What if...

All these thoughts fill my head
But again, no, I can't go back

To a miserable, sickening place
Where my mother is a cold-hearted case

I have to be strong, independent and brave
I will not be treated as a slave
I take a breath of freedom
I take a breath of freedom
This is a journey I'll never forget

I can finally wander around
And hear the beautiful sound
Of nature and trees dancing in the wind
I feel the breeze against my skin

I finally socialise and have a voice
I finally have a voice
I can speak freely
I am not held back
Well not anymore
And I will never be held back again

I am finally free
I am free.

Oluwanifemi Tolufase (12)

The Straying Lamb

With the cross clasped in interlocked hands
I look up to the altar from my seat on the pew
Oh heavenly mother, what I wouldn't do to hear from you...

What am I here for, the purpose of life?
Am I here to live, or to die on God's knife?
My father is poor, my brother is sick
Oh please, when he goes, may God make it quick.

God does not listen, he hears not my cries
My worship will end on the day my brother dies
Does that make me guilty of heresy, of sin?
I'm praying, Mother, but I doubt heaven shall ever let me in

Will I question my faith as I'm stood at the gate?
As I'm begging God to help me see straight?
Mother, Father, why am I here?
Is it wonder? Is it fear?

As I question you, your son, his love
I feel my feathers fading; a crow tearing apart the dove.
The darling, the lamb, staring in shock as a cross
Falls from its shaking lock

There is no father, no shepherd, to steer me back on track
The devil wins and my faith starts to crack
But know this, Mother, I really did try
God, look at me please, see as I begin to cry

Mother
Mary.

Father
God.

Please.
Help.

Help the straying lamb find her way back to the track.

Keisha Lehrle (16)

White (Wine) Lies

Splashed out on the bottle,
The first thousand times.
Cheap wine's now my champagne;
You thought it was a sign.
Pretty white teeth became,
Pretty white lies:
"I'll be chasing that innocence,
For the rest of my life."

And here I am, heartbroken,
Way too scared to toast,
Because if I take a sip,
I'll be 'swept from the coast'.
Drowning in Dom Perignon,
I 'poured the gasoline',
You say I'll never float back up,
'Cause my clothes aren't clean.

I can't sit still at parties,
Forcing salt in the wound.
Your drunk friends are laughing at both,
A clown and a fool;
You're looking too, you've had 8 shots too much,
The words I think, I'd scream at you,
Though I'll scare the birds away,
But for a man with a broken heart, it's nothing new.

I find it so hard because
The bottles were my blood,
You said, "The answer's not at the bottom."
But is it even in the mud,
Which I ran through to get here?
Those millions of years,
I don't look back in anger, but forward in fear,
'Cause I'm in a state that still brings you to tears.

Wear my shoes or
My ragged clothes:
You refuse to do it,
Not until I've walked the road.
Because what is your life,
If not sparkling clean?
I've always cursed the anthem,
'Cause you're no queen.

Beatrix Maspat (13)

Eye Shadow

Looking into the eyes of the boy,
I see eyes good and evil.

I see him building an appearance as if he was a puzzle.
I see his conscious drought of when he looks into the mirror,
I see him hoping the complexion of his splintering face has changed.
I watch over as he begins clawing away at all that is wrong with his face.

No light left in his eyes,
No feeling of joy left in his heart.
This once young and proud boy is hopeless.

I envision the beats of his heart, led on by a thread.
I envision the beacon of light blinding any room he walks through.
I envision a snake shedding its skin,
Slithering through the grass, hiding until sunrise.

I prey on the boy like a hawk, as if he was highlighted.
Even when he is hiding in the crowd, as if he was a ghost,
I see him surrounded by robots, as if they were all a flock of sheep,
Drowned in endless cold-blooded hearts.
I am afraid not even the good can help him of his problems.

At last, I see an eye of gold, glistening in purity and protection, safe of any beast,

I see an eye of mist looming through his mind, snatching memories,
Memories of me and him, together.

This boy is no longer my son.
My boy is lost.

Benji Marshall (15)

The Prison

I arose from my slumber
Realising I lay on a double-decker stone
Engulfed by the shadow of the night
Pain, pain, pain
Dizziness engrossed me
The soreness of my feet, I took a step on burning coal
A voice whispers above
I am frightened, in pain, scared
The figure alights
Vantablack without a face
I am distracted from my predicament.
It hits me, I remember
The whisper: call me Hippocampus.
The strangest name known
Friend or foe, I still have to decide.
A seed of trust develops
I can't comprehend why
It is vantablack without a face
It is Hippocampus in my space
My surroundings; half-painted walls, bars of iron and a flickering lamp above.
I am in prison.
Days on days
Convicted and enslaved
For boredom to die
I try to con

My vantablack inmate
Hippocampus, my frenemy
But I am a hostage
And it seems my taker
I have lost sleep
Perturbed by captivity
Sweating anxiousness
Hippocampus is tranquil
Hippocampus is blameless
My longest quarantine
My longest isolation
Then I discern
It is me, my fantasy, my fabricated world.
I am conflicted by my thoughts
Condemned by my memories
A prisoner of my mind.

Fortune Obasi (17)

Amidst The School's Cruel Gaze

In hallowed halls, where shadows dance,
A heart of thirteen, filled with trance.
Transgender soul, a fragile flame,
Amidst the torment, a whispered name.

Flirting whispers, a cruel jest,
A mockery that pierces their chest.
Their self-harm scars, a hidden pain,
A desperate cry for solace, in vain.

Anxiety's grip, a suffocating hold,
Panic attacks, a story yet untold.
Sensory meltdowns, a chaotic fray,
A world too loud, a mind in disarray.

In the library's embrace, they seek solace,
Amidst the pages, a sanctuary's grace.
Reading's solace, a balm for their soul,
A respite from the torment's toll.

But even here, the burden weighs,
Overwork's chains, a relentless maze.
Tired eyes, a constant reminder
Of the struggles they face, both great and minor.

Yet, amidst the darkness, a flicker of light,
A resilience that shines, despite the night.

They will not be defined by their pain,
But by the strength that they will sustain.

For in the depths of their being, they know
That they are worthy, they will grow.
Transgender and proud, they will embrace their fate,
And rise above the bullies' hate.

Joy Green (12)

Eyewitness Testimony

In the courtroom, they take the stand,
Recalling moments, like grains of sand.
Their words hold power, their memories strong,
But sometimes, perception can be wrong.
Eyes can deceive, memories can fade,
What once seemed clear, now starts to cascade.
Details morph and stories twist,
Truth becomes a fog, hard to resist.

Yet, in the search for justice, we strive
To separate fact from the stories alive.
With caution and care, we must proceed,
For eyewitness testimony is not always what we need.

In the gallery of recall, shadows play,
Witnesses stand in the memory's array.
Their tales unfold like pages worn,
Yet within the mind, a twist is born.
Eyes bear witness to scenes untold,
But memory's fabric can slowly fold.

False echoes dance in the corridors,
Shaping stories with uncertain doors.
Recollections waltz with shades of doubt,
As truth and fiction intertwine, twist and
In the theatre of minds, a subtle ballet,
Where facts and fancy engage in a play.

Witnesses, unwitting orchestrators of tales,
Constructing narrative as memory,
Yet, caution echoes in the silence,
For even truth can wear memory's changing colours.

Khudeeja Begum

Solitary Knight

A lonely knight,
Withering away with no monarch to defend,
He glances from beyond his disgraced castle,
And watches the seasons pass in a silent trance.

The knight is cold,
He is isolated and alone,
Bearing the burden of solitude.
He wants to feel the warmth
Of a companion's loving embrace.

A lonely knight
Defends an empty throne,
No monarch or princess,
Just a distant dream of love.

The knight is bound by eternal chains of remorse,
But he is tethered by the grave sins of his past,
His hands, stained with innocent blood and heinous crimes,
Have made the knight come to realise
Love is nothing but a facade of reality -
But the knight still dreams of a delusion.

He gazes into the mirrored river,
Confronting the reflection of his remorse.
Knowing his stained hands will never be washed clean -
But the knight still dreams of a delusion.

The knight is a strong warrior,
With nothing but an empty throne to defend,
A warrior without purpose, without pride,
Only his longing for love.
A mere flicker of hope in a sea of despair,
Nothing but a distant dream
That refuses to fade.

Daniel Sokunle (15)

The Hurricane

When this raging, fearful
darkness of havoc
storm drifts by as I'm in my room...
When I close my eyes...
I hear every drop of blood,
every scream and
every teardrop from the shadows...

It feels like...
I'm alone in a dark room
with every person who has been
slaughtered
surrounding me...
It doesn't leave me!
A mind-filling thought of
this abomination
destroying my home...
my life!
My family
will be gone!

If I was out there,
I would be dead in a second!
As I watch the peace turn into
hell depression
and a heart-tearing typhoon
that steals the only thing I care about,

my home...

This storm is as strong as
Hercules himself!
This can turn a home
into a ruin!
The wind is howling like a werewolf.
A hurricane is the definition for death...
I see everyone get crushed,
flattened by the remains of
a house.

I can tell barely anyone survived
that day,
I feel sad for their loss
and their painful death
and injuries
I can still hear the screams,
the howling and blood leaking
bodies from that night!

Reggie Saunders (11)

Whispers In The Darkness

In shadows deep, where moonlight weeps,
A child's eyes, where sorrow creeps.
I watched my world collapse in fright,
As darkness fell, extinguished light.

My brother torn, a hostage's plight,
My family's cries, a chilling sight.
In silence, I whisper to the sky,
Beneath the stars, where angels fly.

"O' God above, hear my plea,
Grant solace to my family.
Guide my brother through the night,
Bring back the dawn, restore his sight."

With trembling hands, I cling to hope,
Amidst the chaos, I learn to cope.
Though tears may fall, and fears may rise,
My faith endures, beneath the skies.

In every prayer, a whispered plea,
For peace to reign, for hearts to see.
In the shattered ruins of my past,
I find the strength to hold steadfast.

Through grief and pain,
I find my voice,

Injustice faced, I make my choice.
To rise above, to stand up tall,

In the face of darkness, I stand in awe.
For in my heart, a fire burns bright,
A beacon of hope, a guiding light.
Though broken, scarred, I carry on,
A testament to courage, in the dawn.

Aimal Waqas (12)

Nothing

The universe is vast and empty: filled with nothing.
We are nothing but a spectacle in this little speck of dust we call Earth.
Our lives are insignificant: so much that whether we may die or live holds no concern.
We are nothing. We don't matter.
Nothing truly matters.

But why?
Why?
Why do we stand here?
What significance do we hold?
What is our purpose: fame, wealth, power, worship?

When the stars are out of reach
And we hold no power over our destiny and fate,
When control over our lives loosen
And we spiral mindlessly down the well of despair.

But why?
Why do we matter?
Are we special?
Or is it all just a facade made into a fairy tale to feel loved?
What is love, but a ploy played by Cupid?
Who shoots his arrows mindlessly, creating a disarray of chaos.
Is love not that which leads to hatred and war, depriving us of our sanity and killing our only home?

We are truly nothing;
Relative to the universe, infinitely nothing;
A nothing that does not matter;
A vessel of delusions;
Fuelled by greed, power, wealth, and spiteful love;

A spectacle on a lone planet.

Abobaker Ahmed (15)

Laika

Who are they to send me to this unexplored place?
This dark and scary place that they call space,

Not for a second do they think to be kind,
Or ask a polite question like, do you mind?

And can you believe the reason they're sending me there?
Because it's too scary for their mind to bear,

They don't think, oh dear,
May Laika find this a fear?

Could she be tossing and turning in bed?
Those scary dreams that go through her head?

You think I care about humans' curiosity,
Or for a second, I thought I'm making history?

Five, four, three, two and one,
My sight of my world, in seconds, it's gone,

I'm flying at an incredibly scary speed,
All this for some humans' greed!

I felt like screaming, I'm ready to shout,
What is this all about?

As the rocket was falling down to the ground,
They opened the doors and guess what they found?

They'd murdered the dog that they sent to space,
Get down on your knees and beg for my grace!

I wonder if for even a second you cared,
For the pain and suffering I had to bear.

Yvetta Dixon (12)

Cherry Blossom Tree

Dedicated to Miss Agerbaek, inspiring English teacher - keep doing what you do. Thank you so much!

We danced on London Bridge,
Under the beautiful cherry blossom tree,
Happy as we were,
The sweet cherry blossoms swaying over us as the sun went down,
And in the distance

Over London Bridge, I see
The beautiful cherry blossom tree,

But then all light in my life went out,
A birthday candle blown out in the wind,
Shadows surrounding me and pulling me in,
Yet I still see her everywhere,
In disbelief that that candle will never be relit,

And over London Bridge, I see
The dying, shrivelled cherry blossom tree,

A storm is raging inside and out,
Thunder and lightning,
Snow and sleet,
And the lightning from this all great storm
Lights a spark, destroying everything in raging flame,

And over London Bridge, I see
The burning cherry blossom tree,

In the night,
I shiver not from cold,
I cry not from sadness,
I only long to be whole, to be born from the ashes,
If I only knew how it felt to be whole again,

And over London Bridge, I see
The burnt, charred cherry blossom tree,

In the morning, I wake,
After the storm,
And I realise,
After the flame failed to be properly extinguished,
Life can grow from the ashes,

And over London Bridge, I see
The beautiful cherry blossom tree,

Life can grow again from the ashes of the fire.

Dora Bonner (12)

Palestine

How can I live without my family,
Who were killed by our enemy?
Baba was killed because he tried to show
Everyone in the world what war does, so they know
What goes on and on in our land,
So they shot him, and with his blood on their hands,
They beat my big brother, Ahmed, who tried to defend him,
Then tortured Mama, tearing her limb from limb.
Little Nadin was starved to death,
Her thin, stick-like body, so fragile as she uttered her last breath.
And newborn baby Lamia was so small,
In an incubator, she suffocated, I heard her bawl,
Her shrill, loud shrieks, crying for Mama to feed her,
Without power and supplies, what could he do, the doctor?
Our house is torn to shreds by the bombs and explosives,
Why do they do this, for they have no motives?
How can they kill all these innocent lives?
And starve us and beat us and spray tear gas in our eyes?
I see them doing this every single day,
When will help finally be on the way?
I just want the world to know my name,
I am Jannah, age 13,
I am constantly hungry, alone and fearful,
Watching my country demolish, forever tearful.

The world must know this terrible life of mine,
And many others, for I live in Palest - *Bang!*

Nusaybah Bint-Khalid (13)

A Sister's Fear

Every day was the same, over and over again
Same nights wondering, would he come home?
The hurt you feel as a sibling, as brutal as a battlefield
He left serving the country, I was left to pick up the pieces of a family broken
A sister's worst fear

We live while he is stuck in this cycle day after day
Repetitive, so repetitive
We live every day free, he fights for his life, it's not fair
He needs to be home
Every day, I wake up thinking is he still here? He's not
A sister's worst fear

Think back to the days of childhood
We had freedom, no fear of anything, now filled with a plague of it
What will he bring back, the memories of the things he had seen?
Will he be different? How would I help?
A sister's worst fear

All these questions running through my mind like bullets
He'd been gone 2 years, what if he really wasn't coming back?
These were my worst fears, what if I had lost my brother to war?

He had come back, just not in the way anyone would have wished for him to
My brother was gone. Forever.
A sister's worst fear.

Grace Sampson (17)

Illusions Of The Mind

Deteriorating into a spiral of iniquity,
psychosis drained the sanity from my head
leaving a void of paranoia.
Monomania ruled my thoughts
with sinful delusions, blinding me from normality.
Deprivation of freedom held me captive
in my own mind.
I'm a prisoner
confined in a pit of overbearing corruption,
reflecting our descent into lunacy.
Perhaps the mask of shattered memories
and a plethora of abhor
disguises this hollowness within.
Dejection and despair course through
this lifeless carcass I have become
as if I'm a puppet
controlled by the voices rooted deep in my past.
An incurable wound
bleeding with the trauma of this pitiful life.
The outside of me
shows that of another pointless number of society,
a victim of civilisation
but the inside is a contortion of delirium
and dissoluteness,
strangling any sense of mind
until the torture and suffering burns out.

The pain of my thoughts
driving me to an unspeakable state of paralysis,
consumed by the nightmares deep within.
Darkness won.

Devon Oakes (14)

In The Gas Chamber

We march,
Well, that's what Shmuel had told me when I asked,
We marched 'til we reached grey, monotone houses.
These men, soldiers, I think, shoved us into one of the grey houses,
I saw some young girls about mine and Shmuel's age,
They were crying, strange, I thought we were getting out of the rain,
Then we heard a deafening *click!*

Then in the middle of the room, I saw a hole appear,
Daylight shot in, only for a moment though,
A can was dropped in through that hole,
Most people ran towards where the light had appeared,
Me, Shmuel and a couple others didn't,
Some of the others, though, ran to the walls and scratched at them,
The sound that came from it was like fingernails on a chalkboard.

In the dark, I could feel Shmuel's breath on my cheek,
The air had become toxic,
I struggled for air,
Then, did Shmuel fall to the ground,
I tried to say something, but the air choked me,
The soldiers on the outside were silent,
A little snicker here and there but nothing else,

I fell to the ground next to my only true friend,
Now all I could think about was...
Mummy and Daddy...

Amelia Longhurst (13)

Where Do I Go, Where Do I Stand?

I shall be tough they say
Or I am no man
But where do I go?
Where do I stand?

Men, machinery bombs and traps
Bones, muscles, minds and maps
The sound of gunfire filling the air
As I navigate the battlefield with utmost care.

Down the fields, I hear men roar,
In vociferous cries
Oh wait, here comes more.

Turning over to a restless night
With hope in my heart and courage as my guiding light
Clouds drifting camouflaging the setting sun
Just maybe, this is my time to run.

As the enemies draw near, doubt fills my mind
Is this it?
Is everything over?
A questioning soul, seeking answers to find.

No! No! It can't be
I must stand with hope and humanity
I'll hold my head high and let my thoughts drift away
To memories of loved ones, so far yet so near, I pray

I long for peace, for a world without strife
Where love and compassion can heal a wounded life.

But where would I go?
Where would I stand?
Soldiers are falling
Man after man.

Alyssa Muir (13)

The Species Of The Markhor

Trot as I do, without being noticed,
In my mountains, never have I been seen,
But, what is this?
Food all laid out, amongst all the green.

Perhaps food will come easy today,
Something picks up speed, but I ignore,
I get hit, and now humans have come to whisk me away,
I try to flee, but the sharp wire makes my horns all sore.

Through their eyes,
They have done something wondrous,
Through my eyes,
They have behaved like an ignoramus.

Hustled I am, into a van,
I glare at one, he slaps my head
This human with me, acting like a typical caveman,
As a warning, he picks up a packet of lead.

Maybe they'll take me to the zoo, I thought,
But then, a clatter of guns gave me pure dread,
My hopes of living were painfully cut short,
They will take my horns, my pride, off my head.

My horns, then my fur, then me altogether,
The prison drives on,

I am tied cruelly to a tether,
The lunatic beside me gives a horrifying yawn

O' humans, what are you making us endure?
You will make an end of us,
The Species Of The Markhor.

Anabia Imran (12)

The House That's Lost To Time

If someone peeked through the fence
or drove past the gates outside,
they couldn't even tell that
I'm the house that's lost to time.
I'm a structure for the ages,
though my gardens grow frail and rot,
my rooms are built on memories
too precious to be forgot.
I've hosted endless glamorous feasts
and Gatsby-style soirees,
priceless paintings featured once
on these walls that now decay.
I've been a home for generations,
I've watched loved ones come and go.
Candles and angels once adorned
these trees that no longer grow.
My fireplace roared with golden flames,
it now stands cold as ice;
My piano once sung glorious songs,
now not a song in sight.
These paved paths were meticulous,
now they're coarse and overgrown;
these halls that once were walked with care
lie abandoned and unknown.
And here I'll end my nostalgic tales
of long-gone glory days,

though before you return to real life,
I have one thing more to say -
Treasure every moment,
look around you, not behind,
and don't forget your faithful friend,
the house that's lost to time.

Lucy Shanks (15)

The City Of Blood

There it was
I'd seen enough
As I walked through the city of blood

Rivers of red flowed east to west
Agonising screams, cries of unrest
And as I walked on paths stained with pain
I thought: from this hell, what could anyone hope to gain?

Insides out on broken roads
Shattered windows, reminisces of bone
Piles of rubble and bodies and home
Left to rot in this desert land, all alone

Day and night, unease and tension
Mother nature impaled, practically dead in this dimension
There is no more to it, only less
Was this from God but a deadly test?

A moment of silence for this crumbling land
To think: was this really the work of man?

I pray for rain to wash their bloody hands
But know the blood they spilt has sent innocent people under the sand
I pray for rain to clean this bloody land
But know nothing can wash away the suffering at hand

There it was
I'd seen enough
As I walked through the city of blood.

Asiya Akhtar (15)

Eleftheria: My History

Take our hair and skin and language
Rip our history - take half
Demonise them and that's unfair
Demonise us and nobody cares

The paths in our hair show sight of escape
The paths in our hair in which you erase
The paths in our hair hold gold, seed and grain
'Tis not just hair but our cultural mane

Our skin, our silk and satin cape
With creams of arsenic, mercury we evilly drape
'Tis not just skin but also our pride
But to them, we need to hide

Our hair stands tall with style and power
Ironed flat for us to enter tower
Language vast from many a land
Struck! Banish! Evilly banned

Take our hair and skin and language
Rip our history - take half
Take our mothers, fathers, children from homes
With lies of freedom and riches and curiosity
Shackles, whips, torture and work
No hope. No hope. Starvation... but is there hope?

Take *my* hair and skin and language
Rip *my* history - take half
But word of mouth and songs of slaves
Is something that *you* can't erase.

Chinedum Allanah (15)

Syrian Earthquake

Buildings build up their strength to stay strong and tall
Avoiding surrender, but hope is weakly small
Your office, your school, one after the other, they fall
Everyone watches in shock and dismay, each person in appal

Dig! Dig! Dig under the rubble!
Sweat, burden pain, trying to continue their powerful persistence
Families and their houses, give up in an instant
Nothing can be your protection, not a cheap dwelling, not a luxury residence
All construction demolished, all join in assistance

Dig! Dig! Dig under the rubble!
Confidence and positive spirit is underway
But it gradually decreases, buildings collapse and lie on streets in disarray
Debris on pavements, ruins posing the impression of despair in their own way
Screams, mourns and don't forget the mothers' effortless cries
Dig! Dig! Dig under the rubble!

Violent tremble
Lives at stake

Syria isn't in need of another earthquake
Dig! Dig! Dig, Syrian citizens!
Under piles of rubble.

Talia Kanadil (12)

Perspective

In a fair world, children would walk down the street without fear of discrimination;
fear of being hated on due to the colour of their skin or the shade of their character.

In a fair world, cat-calling is unheard of
and children learn to express themselves without feeling the prowling eyes of predators.

In a fair world... children are hidden from the real world because in the real world: children absorb hateful comments and behaviours like sponges, soaking in every prejudice. Children grow up fearing the inability to get their dream job as others fear what is unknown.

In the real world, even small children exhibit traits of agoraphobia -
they fear the outdoors where once they could express freely.

In the real world, you are not judged by the content of your character
but the case that it is enclosed in.
Like an antique, in the real world,
their value remains hidden inside them waiting to be found.

Teniola Ivienagbor (15)

I, History

Am I a tyrant
Or am I a muse?
Have I abused fates
And led them to their graves?
Or have I shaped them into idolised names?

For I was deprived of freedom when I was just a girl
Dissected by the mortals who dissolved my moments that don't deserve to be told.
Pieces of me are still punctuating the ocean's moans
While some are displayed bare as bones.

My soul is fragmented in galleries of tragedy
And in minds afflicted by agony.
There are parts of me exiled into oblivion
And some consigned to crowds.

My voice evokes texture
And requires humans to venture
To understand the figures they seek and immortalise.

For I, History, render kingdoms in memories
And yet I hound minds until they spiral into insanity
So I will continue to depend on the poets
Who embrace my exposure
And the artists
That bend their brushes and sharpen their chisels to bring me closure.

Amelia Kluk (12)

A Pumpkin

One autumn day,
Without a sound,
A bright orange pumpkin grew out of the ground.
That bright orange pumpkin in the ground was me!
I was the biggest pumpkin you ever did see.

The farmer came to check on the crop,
But when he saw me, the sight made him stop.
For a minute or two, he stared in awe,
Because an enormous pumpkin was what he saw!

He pushed me all the way home, using all his might,
It took him many hours, all through the night.
When the sun rose in the sky,
Something dreadful happened, I thought I would cry!

He made me into stews, cakes and pies,
Many things, because of my huge size.
Hours later, when the sky was its darkest,
He planted my leftover seeds for next harvest.

One autumn day,
Without a sound,
A bright orange pumpkin grows out of the ground.
That bright orange pumpkin in the ground is me!
I am the biggest pumpkin you ever did see.

Zachary Jones (11)

Raindrop

There are many of me, my sisters, brothers
I could never count how many, too many
Life is short, I've been told
I ponder the thought
I've seen them, my sisters, brothers, venture into the outer world
Father lets them free, fly, skydive out of his cloudy body
But I never know where they go next
I ponder the thought
I feel my body sinking from my father's grasp
I guess it's my time to leave
The descent is fast, I see my sisters, brothers
They see me
I see the lush trees, evergreen, passionate
I see the families, happy, together
I see my sisters, brothers, disappearing
I ponder the thought
I land on a transparent medium
I see the child through the display
Happy, interested
It looks at me, my sisters, brothers
Leaning in and slowly dripping
Down, down, down
I ponder the thought
Before plunging into the sea of darkness filled with my sisters, brothers.

Ruby Ahn-Roberts (12)

A Stray Dog's Perspective

As I wander through this busy area,
the cacophony of noises guide me
through the crowd of people.

I watch the tiny beetle scurry
through this unknown world,
while the colossal plane soars above.
Flashes of my owner linger in my mind,
with it brings sadness and joy into my eyes.

As I look at the passing folk,
our eyes lock and their soul speaks to me.
My eyes have seen depression,
they've also seen delight.
My eyes have seen the pain,
they've also seen blessings that come every day.

My eyes have seen the trials,
they've also seen the achievements.
My eyes have seen everyone I loved go away,
they've also seen that love reborn.

I have seen that though our eyes capture all
the hardships and pain,
they also hold the great memories of joy and
blessings along the way.
My eyes are the greatest gift because they show who I am.

Udochukwu Bryan Uhiara (12)

My Vengeful Day

I drift towards the light,
I watch the beams flow around me,
I feel the gentle ring of my collar,
with each small step.
Cling! Clatter! Snap!
Sarah's closed that tatty, old blind,
she's ruined my hourly bird watching.
Scorn begins to spark a flame,
a flame of real spitefulness.
Thud!
I pounce onto the worktop
and promptly begin
eyeing the possible props
for my act -
First the stapler, dark and sharp-tongued,
next the armchair, creamy and forgiving.
Bing!
My eyes shoot a glare
at the now black void on the screen,
silently, I prowl towards the £300 laptop,
I can see the writing
that she says is her 'final essay',
the pointer on a red square.
I click it.

Ruby Howell (13)

Time Capsules: Colours Of Nostalgia

Red and dusty bricks
Green and vibrant ivy
Blue and beautiful flowers.

A garage full of vintage cars and an owner to
Match them too.

A Ford Mustang,
Named as the 'family heirloom' passed from
Their grandfather to them
Made in '69, bought in the same year
Originally black, now turned white.

A Chevrolet Corvette C2,
Painted navy blue
Fitted with bulletproof tyres too,
Many drivers and many passengers from the
Summer of '83 to the winter of '97.

A Mercedes-Benz 380SL,
Bought and made in the 80s
With many memories,
Driven from Canada to California
The history is there to forever stay.

A home office furnished in '87
Added to an old estate built in '56.

Smoke comes from above all around
If it wasn't, it would all be gone,
The whole neighbourhood, abandoned
Broken and bombed.

Matthew Heeks (13)

This Is How The World Works

The most loved dog in the world; a golden retriever,
Not like I am,
An aggressive pit bull,
Being yelled at - "Scram!"
But this is how the world works.

To be loved for who I am,
I'm struggling to learn
How I can ever be another way,
For my whole life, I yearn,
But this is how the world works.

Having so much kindness to give,
In my heart, I am always believed,
No one can tell me otherwise that
I am not who I am perceived as,
But this is how the world works.

"I am truly cared and respected."
You can never relate to me when you say that
"I'm avoided and neglected,"
In truth, I can speak,
But this is how the world works.

Being glared at - "Aww!"
An adorable golden retriever,

Not like I am,
The most hated dog in the world: a pit bull,
This is how the world works.

Jayden Linton (13)

Through His Eyes

It was an eerie, dark night.
Alone in my room.
What should I do?
Just sit in the gloom?
Twenty minutes 'til Dad gets home.

I peered outside, into a distant window.
I saw something move.
Curiosity would say go,
But my dad would say no.
Fifteen minutes 'til Dad gets home.

I went anyway, into that building.
Legs shaking, heart pounding,
Fast breathing, darkness surrounding.
Ten minutes 'til Dad gets home.

I swung open the door, nothing clear anymore.
It was a gruesome sight.
Skin hanging, eyes bulging, a terrifying fright.
Five minutes 'til Dad gets home.

I saw the fear in its eyes, it looked so sad.
It touched my heart, I felt so bad.
I took it home, along the street, all alone.
Two and a half minutes 'til Dad gets home.

Back at home, it's under my bed and over time, a lot was said.
We talked and talked and to my surprise,
I saw his life through his eyes.
Then Dad gets home.

Farrah Bee (13)

Death For The Mighty

The bombs blow left to right
As I try with all of my might
To review my whole life, repent my sins
And pray the Lord would let me in.

Blood stains my succulent hands
As I lose more and more comrades.
One, another, another again
As the enemy gains us in the rain.

Staggering back with weapon in hand
I blindly strike, like a runaway band.
Gurgling, coiling, then now dead
In the sludge, their new deathbed.

Terrain flies past us in a flash
Some bleeding out with an awful gash.
Gasping, choking death once more
More men fall onto the floor.

"Honour, men," the officer cries
As bullets of enemies come whistling by
We charge by night, dead by day
Before the enemy in Milne Bay.

We lie and wait for death to arrive
To be sent forth into the sky.
Honour men, honour for all
Until the mighty who conquer fall.

Emily Kinge (14)

The Tragic Reign Of Anne Boleyn

In the court of Tudor's strife,
Where whispers slice like a dagger's knife,
Anne Boleyn, in her silken grace,
Navigates a perilous, regal chase.

With eyes that gleam like morning dew,
She dances through the courtly brew,
A pawn in power's ruthless game,
Yet a queen in her own fierce flame.

Her heart, a tempest, wild and free,
A longing for love, yet destiny decree,
Caught in the web of Henry's desire,
A throne to ascend, a soul on fire.

Her dreams, once spun in golden light,
Now shadowed by the looming night,
Ambition's price, a heavy toll,
For a crown that weighs upon her soul.

Through whispers, plots, and courtly wiles,
She walks the path of queens and trials,
Yet in her heart, a quiet plea,
For love, for freedom, for destiny.

So let history write its tale
Of Anne Boleyn, who dared to sail,
Through tempests fierce and oceans wide,
A woman's spirit, undenied.

Shyann-Marie Northeast (13)

From Solitude To Symphony: A Pebble's Odyssey

In the heart of the ocean, a pebble lay,
Lost in the vastness, adrift in the blue,
No purpose if found in the ebb and sway,
Just a silent witness to days that flow.

It watched as the waves danced their endless dance,
A solitary soul amidst the sea's sprawl,
Longing for a shore, a place to enhance,
A yearning for connection, for a beckoning call.

Then one fatal day, the currents did guide,
To a rugged coastline, where rocks stood tall,
Amongst a mighty beach, it found its stride,
No longer adrift, no longer small.

Now part of grandeur, a tapestry of stone,
Each pebble and boulder, together they bind,
In unity, they carve, with a purpose known,
A masterpiece of nature in harmony entwined.

No longer alone in the ocean's endless roar,
But part of a chorus, where each voice is heard,
Together they shape the coastline's grand decor,
In unity, they find purpose, each pebble, each boulder.

Joseph Carrothers (15)

Harmony In Battle: Verses Of Unity Amongst Diversity

Amidst the fray, I stand alone,
An Indian soul in a sea of stone.
Soldier's creed binds, yet hearts divide,
In the tumult of battle, I seek to abide.
Through whispered taunts and silent stares,
I bear the weight of unspoken cares.
Each step, each breath, a battle within,
Against the tide of bias, I strive to begin.
In the chill of night, beneath starlit skies,
I find solace in the moon's gentle guise.
With each dawn's light, a renewed resolve,
To rise above prejudice, to steadfastly evolve.
For in this crucible of conflict and strife,
I carve my path with valour, with life.
Though the journey be steep, the path unsure,
I march with courage, my spirit pure.
Through the trials of war, I find my voice,
A beacon of hope in the midst of noise.
For in the depths of struggle, amidst discrimination's art,
I find my heritage in my Indian heart.

Antos Thomas (14)

Drowning

Drowning
Drowning
Pulling you under
Like waves crashing in a stormy night
Gasping for a single breath
But it all pulls you under
Like an anchor
Weighing you to the sea floor

Except you aren't in the sea
You're on land
But the feeling is there
Trying
But barely keeping your head above the waves

The waves may be metaphorical
But the pain is not
So you put on a smile
Hoping one day, it might feel real
But one day is a long shot

Expectations
The silent killer
The waves dragging you under
Drowning you
No matter how hard you try
Try as you might

You're sinking
Being pulled under the waves

You could ask for help
But who could help?
You feel like a failure
Everyone is moving on
Apart from you
Stuck in the sea
Drowning.

Bethany Milner (18)

Mary I - Forgotten

Her sullied feet frozen on the blackened floor
a tarnished crucifix around her neck
as droplets of liquid glass glaze her skin

troubled fears stalk the darkened crevices of her frown
splashes of misery fleck the tarnished canvas
while heaven and hell do watch with steely eyes

he forgave her sins on Sunday morn'
beads of sweat glisten when hands become one
faith doth cast aside her cries

judged by thousands, helped by none
disdain and shame do greet like brothers
and curtains of peace are ripped apart in rage

a cloak of tears shrouds her face
first comforting, then suffocating whilst
ragged talons of sadness choke at the happiness she clutches

a lifebelt, bright and soft, floats in the distance
a beacon of light amidst the sea of darkness
her hand strains, but grasps nothing but air.

Madeleine Fremantle (13)

What Would Life Be Like If...

Sometimes I sit and think to myself,
What would life be like if I was somebody else?

What would life be like if I was popular?
Would I be excited to step foot into school,
To see all my 'mates' and attend the extracurriculars,
Or would it be overwhelming to have to be constantly 'cool'?

What would life be like if I was famous?
Would I love my admiring fans,
To watch edits of myself to the song 'Shameless',
Or would I wish to run away and start a new life in Japan?

What would I be like if I was 'normal'?
Would I proudly speak with confidence,
To not know my morals,
Or would I feel punished and it feel like a consequence?

Sometimes I sit and think to myself,
What would life be like if I was somebody else?
But now I think more,
I think I like my unique self.

Summer Petch (15)

I Don't Like People

I don't like people.
I find them hard to handle,
They can't tolerate each other - what a scandal!
I don't like people.

I don't like people.
They kill, they fight, destroy all light,
I don't like people.

I don't like people.
A brother, a sister,
A Mrs, a Mr.
It doesn't matter,
I don't like people.

I don't like people.
They mimic, they copy,
They distract and get sloppy.
I don't like people.

I don't like people.
My hopes, destroyed by death,
My dreams weaken as I grow short of breath,
I don't like people!

But
When the clouds turn to grey,
When the world's in dismay,

Be the light,
Show the fight,
Make the wrong right,
Be the steeple, even
If you don't like people.

Devon Sandell (13)

Dear Black Girl

Dear black girl, let me tell you,
You're a shining star, strong and true.
Your beauty radiates inside and out,
With resilience and grace, there's no doubt.

Your melanin is magic, a gift so rare,
Embrace your heritage, be proud and share.
Your voice is powerful, let it be heard,
Speak up for justice, let your truth be stirred.

In a world that tries to dim your light,
Rise above, keep shining bright.
You are worthy, you are enough,
Break down barriers, show your stuff.

Dear black girl, know your worth,
You're a queen, a force on this Earth.
Never let anyone define your worth,
You're capable of so much from birth.

So dream big, reach the sky,
You have the power, don't be shy.
Embrace your magic, let it unfurl,
Dear black girl, you can change the world.

Tiarna Forbes (16)

Through The Eyes

Through the eyes, I can glimpse my abundant dreams come to fruition
While she laughs with complete purity
I wait for all the good that will happen to me through the eyes.

Through the eyes, I grasp my imagination, spreading through the deepest crevasses
When my body has surpassed its limits
It's only my mind that carries me...
Through the eyes

Through the eyes, I live, love and laugh through the lens of another
As I recover the fallen and vague memories of my youth, I ponder...
Through the eyes

Through the eyes, I long for fate to stroke my hand and give me a chance
So when I give a peerless glance at her, my dream is renewed
Through the eyes

For my eyes have been restored and I can look to the skies once more
Yes, I leave my core to take a giant leap
Through my eyes.

Joshua Oyebanji

A Detective's Mind

As my mind begins to wander
I am stuck on this case
And I haven't got a clue.
Missing bodies stacking up each day
With no lead to lay.

In shadows deep
I tread with care
My eyes alert
My mind aware
Every clue, a silent waltz
Every move, a puzzling mystery
Unravelling the secrets
With a single glance.

Through alleys dim
And streets so cold
I chase the truth
Both young and old.
In silhouettes of the night's embrace
I find light in the darkest of places.

In the heart of the city's beat
I follow leads with steady feet.
Mysteries unravel at my touch
In this puzzle, I find so much.

With my magnifying glass in hand
I search for clues all across the land.
Each puzzle piece, a story untold
In the shadows
The truth unfolds...

Chloe Ramsay (13)

Psychosis

Oh, the struggle
the desire to be mentally insane
red lines and big thighs
not a thought to be sane
oh, the addiction
the fantasy of bright lights, black
hearts, shredded soul, missing parts
oh, the obsession
to be burning in flames, inhaling the
sorrow and the death that we gain
oh, the infatuation
to be in constant pain
the blood, the white
my messed-up brain
oh, the feeling
the sex, the destruction we gain
the love, the pleasure and all of the
pain
oh, the ache
the torture of the mind, the shreds of
the thigh, all the stories and the little
white lies
oh, the temptation
the urges to be something that should
never be seen
oh, the desperation

how I crave the insanity, psychosis of
the soul, never once yet to be whole.

Lucy Walton (18)

Through My Eyes: A Chimney Sweep

In the days of old, so long ago,
I (a chimney boy) worked; head hung low.
My little hands, blackened and scarred,
Climbing sooty chimneys, life so hard.
From dawn 'til dusk, I'd work away,
Carrying burdens, day by day.
My legs, weary, bearing the weight
Of forty pounds of clay, oh, what a fate!
My feet, injured, sore and worn,
Trudged up narrow chimneys, forlorn.
The soot and grime clung to my skin, yet I climbed, never giving in.
And yet for very little did they pay,
I'd work so hard throughout the live long day.
From six at morning, 'til seven or eight,
My legs had tumbled beneath the weight
Of forty pounds of clay or more,
My feet were sore.
Remember, everyone, as you play, I (a chimney boy) struggle, day by day.
My story reminds us to be kind,
For every child deserves a better find.
And that's the end of my chapter!

Rachel Moulder (11)

Rose-Tinted Glasses

In your eyes, he is everything.
The sparkle in his ocean-blue eyes and the way his golden hair falls perfectly,
In your eyes, he is a work of art.
His face sculpted by God himself.
Oh, how his words compel you,
His sugar-coated lies reciprocated with an innocent smile,
In your eyes, he can do no harm.
The patchwork of bruises lining your skin 'an accident',
The violet beneath your skin glowing a bright hue.
It's your fault, you deserved it.
Soft kisses along your supple skin, soothing the sting beneath,
Your heart aches for more.
'Forgive me' flowers adorn the mantle with a flame burning bright beneath,
Flame.
You were a moth to a flame,
For in your eyes, he loves you, adores you.
Life through your eyes,
A blurred vision through rose-tinted glasses.

Brogan Reilly (17)

Look Through My Eyes And See We Used To Be Friends

We used to be friends before you gave up the act.
We used to be friends before all the rumours and lies.
We used to be friends before the broken promises.
We used to be friends before the jealousy.

We used to be friends before you tore my world apart.
We used to be friends until the late-night fights.
We were friends before all my sleepless nights.
We used to be friends before the death threats.
We used to be friends before the panic attacks.
We used to be friends until I was scared to leave the house.

I used to have friends until I met you.
I used to be confident until I met you.
I used to be happy until I met you.

You should look through my eyes and feel what it is like to be friends with you.
You should see what it is like to be the victim in your story.

Kelsey Coulson (17)

Looking Through The Eyes Of My 26-Year-Old Cat, Whizz

My silky black fur in the sun,
I never chase birds, it isn't fun.
I walk on the roof at the dead of night,
When I poke my head to the window, my emerald eyes will give you a fright.

It feels weird now my claws don't retract,
I'm way too relaxed, I never attack.
I'm still feeling young,
Even if I'm wise and 121.

Telling my owner, I see the light getting bright,
I stare into my owner's eyes and tell myself I always had a reason to fight.

They tell me that it's okay to leave,
I close my eyes and think about us together, and we will both grieve.

But now I have passed, I should go over the rainbow bridge, towards my endless peace,
But I want to be in my owner's arms, feeling their warm and loving release.

Kai Beverton (14)

The Catastrophic Fall Of Athena

One... Two... Three
Through misty fires and smoky swords; will you set me free?
The soldiers march with their clashing chainmail
Yet only one army will prevail
Enduring blistering winds were not a shock
Hell crept in with a knock
Its burning breath snuck in perilously
The soldiers watched incredulously.

Alas, the end is near
This burden of mine is too severe
Hell and I are interlocked
I resist the smouldering chains, but all these lives on the battlefield I can't repay
I seek a conversation with the light
But the sky envelopes itself, so the Gods and I cannot reunite
Fortunately, I am no mortal
But the consequence of nihilism rejects me from entering God's celestial portal

One... Two... Three...

Fatima Hirsi (14)

Beneath The Shadow Of Wealth

In a world full of whispers and jeers,
She walks alone through her fears,
Her worn-out shoes and tattered dress,
She might look like a mess,
But in her heart, a story of agony and pain.

Eyes looking up and down,
Multiple times, starting to frown,
Mocked and teased for what she lacked,
Her heart felt heavy, her confidence cracked.

With each cruel word, her strength shatters,
Would people ever think it matters?
They pointed fingers, they made her cry,
This time, she aimed high.

Her dreams were too big to let her down,
She promised to make her parents proud,
Because one day, she'll make a change,
Her light will shine bright, her stories told,
A little girl who brought love to this world.

Laura Alishat (13)

The Earth

I am your planet
I am your home
I am Earth
A mere mixture of water and land
I create trees
Only for them to be cut down
By the very people I let live on me
I gave them a home
I gave them oxygen
Instead of caring and looking after me
They cause pollution and deforestation
Destroying me bit by bit
Destroying my beloved creations
They disrespect me
By throwing rubbish in the sea
Killing innocent sea animals
Melting icebergs and glaciers
Animals in the Arctic are losing their homes
Faster than a tree can lose all its leaves
I used to be a perfect planet
Until climate change took reign
Now I'm overheating
Hot is overpowering cold
Save me now or never
For your planet.

Mya Das (11)

Timothy The Turtle

I was all right until they came along,
In fact, I was happy, but still a bit snappy,
I travelled to their house, it took an hour long,
And what can I say? They were very chatty!

They put me in a bathtub, on the top floor,
And gave me some bread and lettuce and more,
Then something happened that I'll never forget,
They left me on the balcony, it became a downpour!

So, I huddled in my shell, as lightning struck again,
My heart began to race as the storm thundered on,
Minutes, hours passed - they must be insane!
I thought of my family, and my dad, Ron.

After that night, the best ever thing happened,
They took me home and back to my father,
I was so happy, I felt safer, then gladdened,
So, what do you think? I'm now much smarter and calmer!

Cynthia Guo (12)

Whispers Of Fading Memories

In the shadows of my mind, I roam,
Lost in a labyrinth I call home.
Memories like whispers, fleeting, dim,
Fading echoes of a life once brim.

Faces blur like watercolour in rain,
I grasp at fragments, but find only pain.
Names slip away like ships at sea,
Lost in the vastness of my memory.

Time unravels, a tangled thread,
Moments slip through fingers, fled.
I wander aimless, in a world unknown,
A ghost of who I once had known.

Yet in the quiet, amidst the haze,
A flicker of light, a gentle blaze.
Love's warmth, a beacon in the night,
Guiding me through the endless flight.

Though the shadows may obscure my view,
In the depths of my heart, I still hold you.
For though my mind may drift away,
My love for you will always stay.

Rayana Itakhunov (16)

A Pen

Sometimes, I wish that I could be free

Stuck in a case, no liberty for me
Suffocating heat, it's so hard to breathe
Rarely to see the light of day
Will things always be this way?

Will they ever do me a favour
Of sparing the wrath of book or paper?
My insides drain out, used as ink
Soon I will die, I'm on the brink

Humans are cruel, mindless monsters
They treat me like I am something worthless
They claim to be compassionate, are they really?
They clearly do not say this sincerely

This cannot go on, it just isn't right
We need to bring the issue into their sight
Then they will understand that it is real
All their dark secrets, we will reveal.

Ayinza Igaga (11)

How I Think My Cat Acts When I Hug Him

I sit patiently on the windowsill,
As the sun rays reach out to find me.
I hear the birds chirping and singing,
As her mum begins to clean and tidy.

I'm connecting to the nature that I sense,
Beyond these walls, beyond the glass.
Beyond where nobody has been before,
Beyond where you have the finest grass.

The eerie noise of the vacuum ruins it all,
Then I lick my paws, my leopard fur glistening.
I make one, only one sudden movement,
Yet, I know that now she is listening.

I brace myself for the 'unnecessary' hug,
As she rushes into the room, stroking my head.
There are other places I'd rather be...
But, I'll just enjoy this hug instead.

Farah Karim (11)

All Around Me

Lights, voices, music
It was plainly enough - enough!
My vision was blurry
My eyes wandered off -
As my breathing quickened.

Nasty comments got to me
"Leave me be!"
Glares, I got as a response
These emeralds flickered everywhere -
Strayed off to nowhere

My pace accelerated as I stood upright
The world was spinning, I was definitely going insane!
A familiar snow-white cage appeared
Snapping my head around like an owl
I was not looking sage

Everything paused for me
Spiteful, mischievous, venomous glares stopped
Frowning at my surroundings, I ran
A breeze hit me in a span
The bewitching bird was finally released.

Huen Ting Fong (14)

Aurora Borealis

I am the beauty of the north,
I beat all common lights.
They look at me with awe,
And long to be likewise.

I am the running stream,
Of mauve, emerald, azure.
My aura dazzles the village,
They chase my scenic allure.

I am the fugitive of light.
I watch as you watch for me.
But the minute you finally catch up,
I vanish into the deep.

I am the Northern Lights,
My pride and joy is to dance.
You can come and waltz with me,
If you get the chance.

I am the breath of victory,
The dust of forged metals.
You see me as a spectacular display
But I array the souls of heroes.

Aurora Borealis,
I have many names,
But you can just distinguish me
By my vibrant roaring flames.

Sofia Haacke (14)

The Mind

Waves come as wispy blue-green strands of hair
With the finest hints of gold
From the twisted sun
The hue of the water, ever-changing yet familiar to all
They start off as gentle ripples of shallow water hitting your feet
Until you realise that this, this is not the sea
Instead, it is the thoughts in my mind, not just one thought
But a thought that ticks over like crossing waves
Never one at a time
A silent storm that never sleeps but grows with every passing day
There is a numbness in me that keeps me awake
A pain that drugs won't dissipate
You know it is not the way, I know it is not the way, but...
It is only one hole to sink a ship at the end of the day.

Amelia Nelson (14)

Sometimes

Sometimes when I breathe, it feels like I'm drowning
Sometimes when I walk, it feels like my body is disintegrating
Sometimes when I speak, it feels like I'm eating up my own flesh
Cry has three letters but so does joy
Positivity has ten letters but so does negativity
Worried has seven letters but so does excited
It feels like life gives you a choice
But you get redirected every time
It feels like
Everything I say is wrong
Everything I wear is wrong
Everything I do is wrong
I will never do anything right
You could jump but you'll never reach the moon
You could run but you'll never get across Earth
Sometimes, everything goes wrong.

Victoria Maleki (13)

But Then I Woke Up

There was a time where rays would shine through my window
But then I woke up.
I once played in the park, believing I could fly
But then I woke up.
Dreamed of staying young forever, just me and maybe them
But then I woke up.

You don't stay young forever, despite it being known
You never truly feel such fear until you're nearly grown
I once believed in fairies and monsters in the dark
But then I woke up.

The monsters aren't on the playgrounds yet
Although you will meet them soon
They prey on your insecurities, play in your head just like a tune

I believed I was enough once, happy and full of hope
But then I woke up.

Abbie Pritchard (16)

Odysseus

As Odysseus, I've sailed the boundless sea,
A man of cunning, known in every land.
Through trials dire, my spirit shall be free,
With courage forged by fate's relentless hand.

From Troy's high walls, where war's fierce tempests roared,
To distant shores where dangers lay in wait,
Through sirens' songs and Cyclops' caverns floored,
I navigate, driven by my fate.

But in my heart, a longing ever burns
For Ithaca, my dear and cherished home,
Where Penelope's love patiently yearns,
Amidst the waves where endless roam.

Oh, may the Gods grant me the strength to see
My journey's end, and find my destiny.

Harmani Dhaliwal (16)

Control

Door widens. The gates of hell have narrowly opened.
The fires of hell peek through this slender opening.
Fire expeditiously comes and burns me.
It hurts, yet this pain comforts me in the way of life.
That pain causes me to doubt who to love and adore.
Who should I trust and where should I belong?
These gates of hell bind me in the shackles of time.
Where freedom isn't close and neither is it far.
Time holds; I hold on longer.
As with time, it brings worse pain than I have ever felt.
This feeling I have to bear.
As with time, it brings pain.
This pain I don't want to bear.
But with time becomes pain,
And this pain is inevitable.

Rainé Bennett-Rawlins (15)

Immortal Infant

From craftsmen's hands, I took my form:
a babe of bronze with no uniform.
Cast in fires of a worktable's delight,
I gleamed with bronze in the Grecian light.

In the fire's arms, I once did lay,
adorned with laurels, allowed to play,
a token of love, a cherished prize:
I saw the world through infant eyes.

In ancient hands, I was adored,
A symbol of a bygone, never deplored.
But tireless time took its toll...
and now I lie: a glass-bound soul.

No longer do I feel the breeze,
or hear the whispers in the trees,
or feel the sun's warm kiss,
or taste nature's purest bliss.

But here I am, encased in glass,
just a relic of the prehistoric past.

Coco Blank (14)

Depression's Eyes

Looking through depression's eyes,
Everything is so dark and dull.
Nothing ever seems to change,
Everything that others feel,
My depression eyes make unreal.
The bright sun in the mornings,
My mind identifies as a storm.
The colourful flowers and fruit-filled trees
Never seem to look alive for me.
I have never really understood the weather
And how it is supposed to make you feel,
But my thoughts are like a hurricane,
But I guess that's just the devil's deal.
Everything is so dark and dull,
Looking through depression's eyes.
Everyone thinks the cold is the monster,
But I think it's my mind.

Casey Clarkson (16)

Extinct

Life was great.
Life was peaceful.
We had a source of food,
A place to shelter,

Until they came.

They were smart,
They shouldn't have been a threat,
Had strange, dangerous objects,
We were now their prey.

They made us rugs,
Hung our heads upon a wall,
Ate us for dinner,
Kept us in cages for show.

The life we once knew,
Disappeared from the world,
One by one,
Our species was extinguished,
Like a flame in the water.

If only then they knew
The damage they did,
But today, it still continues,
For we are now labelled

Extinct.

Charlotte Easter (11)

Blobfish

I spend my time huddled among the rocks
The water is especially cold this year and I find myself
Alone in this empty place
You come to visit me, all the way down here
Bringing your glaring lights and your incomprehensible machines
I see you, you don't belong here

You ask me to join you, I listen to your tales
Of land and light and lush greenery
As you drag my body to the surface, I see so many
New beautiful things

I wish I could see more, I'll fall apart trying
Your pretty world isn't meant for me
I'll never know it, a mangled shape will be all
You have to remember me.

Oliver Daniel (15)

The Obsolete IWB

The class looked intently at the picture I presented
I liked doing that; it made me contented
I felt a never-ending sense of joy
Building up inside me like I was playing with a toy
A burst of laughter
I felt I shan't be hereafter
I realised my fate
To be swapped with a blank slate...

The image was displayed
With a sigh of dismay
I knew my time was coming
To be replaced
I knew my life was ending
With another sigh
I drew my last breath
And then I died.

I was thrown into the dumpster
With a big bang and crash
My corpse lay in silence
And that was that.

Lucas Knibbs (13)

The Eyes Of Those Who Give

I tie my hair,
Slip on my gloves,
Push the door open,
Ready for combat.

She lies there, lifeless,
Around her,
Consultants,
Junior medics,
Nurses,

Chest compressions,
1
2
3
No luck.

Defbrilliator,
I yell,
Glassy eyes stare back at me,
Delivering shock in...
3
2
1

A low hum fills the room,
Beep!
Beep!

Beep!
And I breathe too.

A breath that many weren't able to take again;
But a breath this lady could,
Thank you, she whispers

And suddenly -

It all makes sense,

The role of a nurse isn't only to give,
But receive moments like this too.

Tumi Ajibola (14)

Through Granny's Eyes

A distant glance
A frightening trance
A never-ending story
They supposedly call glory
A punishment or discipline
Taking away my underpin
My family gone, my friends dead
My country, from which I fled
Repaying my lawful debt to God
Doesn't this just seem odd?
And I can't reach out for help
My life's the water and I'm the kelp
I don't want to make them worry
'Cause all they would say is sorry
Sorry you weren't here with me
Sorry you lost two and I lost three
Sorry my voice echoes around my empty house
Sorry that my heart is now the size of a mouse.

Carli Zinzani (12)

Lost In Music

I am getting ready to perform,
I place my fingers on the piano keys,
I feel myself burning in the spotlight,
But then I start to play with ease.

I'm immersed in my own world,
Playing an uplifting tune,
The rest of the world stops to listen,
While the melody rises up to the moon.

I feel so happy and hopeful,
Everyone else watches in awe,
I am completely lost in the moment,
And my heart starts to soar.

The piece is now coming to an end,
I feel so proud of what I've achieved,
A warm smile spreads across my face,
As I play the final note on the keys.

Yasmin Ballard (11)

The Plea Of The Solanum Lycopersicum

I stare at my ruddy skin,
flushed with embarrassment,
slick with tears.
Yet another argument about me.
About where I belong.
About how I do not belong.
All the while,
misunderstood,
as my vowels are mispronounced.

I profess my love with flowers,
and present you
with life itself,
in little ivory droplets.
But you chastise me
for my simplicity and honesty.
Bitter and frugal.
Neither fruit, nor vegetable.

Spiky green. Smooth red.
An overwhelming clash
between what you wish me to be
and what I shall remain.
Beyond botanical categories,
beyond possibilities.
Laid bare before you.

Please accept me
as just a tomato.

Ayooluwamide Oluwole (16)

The Baby Bird

I perch on a branch
That rests so high,
I then look up
Because I want to fly.

I flap my wings,
I try and try,
Yet I fall back down,
And want to cry.

I watch my friends,
How they whirl through the air,
I'm desperate inside,
But pretend not to care.

I try again,
I flap so hard,
I can't give up now
When I've come so far.

I lift an inch,
Then a couple more,
I can't be stopped now,
I'm free to soar!

I join my friends,
We fly away,
It's so much fun,
What a wonderful day!

Sophia Clayton (13)

I Experienced It All

I saw it all, I saw the tears
The saddened tears on saddened peers

I felt it all, I felt the whip
The whip that through our skin could rip

I smelt it all, I smelt the rust
The rust that formed a bloody crust

I heard it all, I heard the screams
The screams infected peaceful dreams

I tasted it all, I tasted the chains
The chains that trapped us in disdain

I lived through it all, I lived through the pain
The pain of being treated like an unwanted stain

So I wished for it all, I wished for a day
A day with no such thing as a slave.

Gaïa Renverse Harris (12)

The Unknown

It was unknown if she could see me
It was unknown if she could hear me
I couldn't tell if it was my imagination
Or if it was in her own creation
I felt the weight come down on my head
Or was I just a bit misled?
I could see her approaching now
Will she notice me somehow?
I will be used for the first time in an era
Or would I just have to hold her mascara?
Would I be drenched?
And then her fist would be clenched
As the glass smashes
She says that things like these happen
But then I think I am always under the influence
Of dreams that feel like reality.

Reuben McKenna (14)

Grey-Blue

Grey walls,
Thin light fading through the window,
Bouncing off grey books and grey plants,
With a dulling blue glow,
Late nights fuelled by coffee,
Bright screens glossy,
Bosses bossy,
But,
Brain cells dying,
Stress multiplying,
People prying,
And no one's denying
That all this work, all this stress,
Will amount to nothing, nevertheless,
And even though I try and try,
I can't help but deny and cry,
And admit that this is tiring,
Even though I am inspiring
All my family and all my friends,
This numbing torture never ends.

Alice Dubroeucq (13)

Childhood

We have grown up too fast, left everything
Childhood memories we rarely unlock
Those times we will never get back, nothing
We have been deprived of our empty talk
Confused, loud, and curious we had been
Now social media is in our head
We must have clear skin and our body thin
We cannot appear sad or tears be shed
But growing up is just a part of life
Something we must accept, despite our fear
We must be in the present all our life
We only live once, our life must have cheer
Seizing the moment and not looking back
Is what our childhood self would want so bad.

Grace Jackson (12)

Hamster

As a hamster, I spin round and round, so quiet you can't hear a sound.
My tiny paws make me, which I'm proud of, I love being me.

I stuff my cheeks with food galore. It's really good, I'd love to have more!
As I drink my water, it feels good. And then I go dig in the bed shavings of wood.
My body is plump, fluffy and cute, running in circles without dispute.

When I get tired, I curl up in a ball and sleep for an hour, maybe more!
Sometimes my owner takes me out to play, maybe I could leave a little surprise on my way.
I'm a little ball of happiness, energy, and glee, this is why I love being me!

Adele Bagdonas (11)

Flawed

All around, there is red,
The glee and hope have fled,
Noises that once were quiet,
Grow louder, louder yet,
The things that were so rational,
Just do not make sense at all.

Your favourite perfect picture,
Shatters like glass on the floor,
Why is there a need to be perfect?
Why cannot people accept their flaws?
Or is perfection like a law?

Some people are mixed and matched,
But outcast like a bad batch,
Some people are better for it,
Stronger to step out the door,
The person you saw as flawed
Is just as perfect as before.

Amaoge Okoli (16)

WWII Soldier

W e run from the Germans
O ver the hills, over the mountains
R un, run, run
L eader tells us to fight but we are double outnumbered
D own the mountains, down the hills

W e set up our positions
A re we actually doing this?
R eady, steady

S hoot!
O ur men and their men go down
L ots of blood and tears
D own and down, more and more men
I n the battle, every lost friend
E nd of the battle, Germans win but it's not over
R ussians are coming.

Lewis Cross (12)

The Replacement

An endless sea of possibility
Pixels, portraying life within me
Click, snap, wipe, all in your imagination
Like a field of flowers, I sway gently with vibration.

Sadly, my emotions, I can't portray
Just like a needle in a stack of hay
Smashed vigorously, thrown aggressively, I could hear my owner say
It's a machine, it can't feel the pain

Every message, every snap, dinging back to back
Suddenly, a new phone appeared, was I sacked?
It shimmered brightly, quickly with glee
With my last breath, I could see, my owner replaced me.

Rustam Ofarinov (13)

President Of America

P resident of America
R emarkable really
E veryone watching you
S eeing what you will do
I n front of everyone
D on't mess it up
E ducated on what to do
N ever your own decision
T hey decide for you

O f course, it's great
F eeling that power

A merica gave it to you
M any will try to kill you
E xhale when it's done
R elax for a moment
I n the peace you gained
C ards revealed
A ssassination.

Ewan Jones (17)

Dancing Angels

Dancing is a journey,
A journey only I can see,
Watching and waiting for the things I may be.

Within the music and bright lights,
You saw me dancing, night after night,
With my whitewashed wings and pointed ballet shoes,
Dancing with nothing to lose.

Across the world, you sent me far and wide,
To dance where we had nothing to hide,
"The first ballerina to dance around the world," they used to say,
Or as I saw it, a game to always play.

Dancing cannot be forgotten,
It is the journey that lives within me,
Waiting and whispering for the things I may be.

Sasha Green (17)

A Final Verse For The Dying

No one around to hear your cries.
No one around, you are left to die.
Your friends lie, glass-coated eyes.
Not one of them to survive.

The darkness surrounding,
The blood oozing.
No backup.
No escape.

You stop resisting,
You let the darkness take over.
All hope is lost.
You cough and splutter.
You can't breathe,
You are drowning in the darkness.
You are drowning in regret.

One last glimpse
At who used to be your friends.
One last glimpse
At the decrepit battlefield.
One final glimpse
Of the natural daylight
Before the darkness takes over.

Hallie Whitmore-Bond (13)

Empty Eyes Of A Rotting Bear

The sun is bright
It is warm on the leg, exposed to the light
Tomorrow will be a rainbow
I can feel the humidity start to grow
My arm aches, matted and lean
It is sprawled over my chest as it always has been

Someone opens my prison, lets the sun find me
I do not see them. My sockets are empty

They walk like she used to
She will clean me, she must do
There is something alive growing under my arm
But then she comes closer and shouts in alarm
Running out, she slams the door
I rot a second more.

Michelle Croll (13)

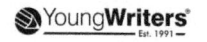

Be Yourself

You may think I'm boring
But at least I'm spending time with the people I love
You may think I have no money
But instead, I'm trying to save up

You may think I'm lonely
But at least I don't have fake friends
You may think I'm smart
But at least I'm not failing

You may think I am annoying
But at least I am entertaining

Why don't you leave me alone?
Why do you have to come to me?
Are you jealous?

Be yourself
Be yourself
Be yourself.

Ruqayyah Ajmal (14)

Grow Wild

At the crack of dawn,
I fly across the dewy lawn.
Searching for the perfect flower,
Before the clouds let out another shower.

But the perfect flower is hard to find,
Because the farmers do not mind
That the colony is dying.
Pesticides keep bugs away, no matter, we keep trying.

Our sweet, sticky honey
That you will take to make money.
We do a lot more than you would think.
Without us, you humans would rapidly shrink.

What can you do? My dear child,
Just let your garden grow wild.

Ellinea Boiling (14)

I Am Amonute

How can I author my story if it no longer belongs to me?
They give me the pen they stained with colony, but it refuses to dance with my unfamiliarity.
I try to set fire to their book, yet it is glazed with a white man's privilege.

They tell me I'm free, but I am captured for his sensuality.
They tell me I'm loved, but they stole my infantility and repay me with a corrupted youth.
They tell me I am brave, whilst a distortion of my legacy lives on.

They tell me I am Pocahontas, but I am Amonute.

Yanet Teklu (17)

Wake Up To Reality

I was moulded by the light
I am immortality
I am guidance
You were moulded by the dark
You are depression
You are unloved

I am a diamond
I am valuable
You are a rhinestone
You are a dummy pretending to be someone

I am a theory
I am what things should be
You are reality
How things are

I am a cure
I am a second chance
I am relief
You are a disease
You are unwanted
You are despised

I am your dream
You are my reality.

Kamran Mughal (17)

The Wildfire

It started on a normal day,
But the sun had other ideas,
The sun wreaked havoc,
The sun created a monstrosity,
The wildfire.

The wildfire was a ravenous blaze,
With an appetite for destruction.

It created thick smoke,
Intoxicating the atmosphere.

It burned down the trees,
Polluting the globe,

Spreading like a contagious sickness,
Slaughtering the peace in the world.

The wildfire has struck.

Maybe next time,
It will come for you.

Henry Duce (14)

Through Their Eyes

Schizophrenia, you have no idea what I would do to live without you.
Your words are in my head, knives in my heart.
You build me up, but then I fall apart.
You are a predator that keeps breaking me apart.
And you are always following me,
And you are always here with me,
And no matter what I do, you will never leave.
I carry on like a soldier with a battle wound, crying out from every thought my body consumes.
But I will never stop fighting,
Because I will be on the winning side of the war.

Victoria Cicha (16)

I'm A Bully

I'm a bully.
I don't know why I'm this way.
I just am.

I'm a bully.
I just feel so angry.
All the time.

I'm a bully.
I'm only joking.
And jokes get laughs.

I'm a bully.
I like seeing people laugh.
It can't be that bad.

I'm a bully.
Why is she crying?
It really is only a laugh.

I'm a bully.
Why isn't she at school?
Why?

I'm a bully.
Maybe this isn't so funny anymore.
I'm a bully.
I'm a bully.

Ava Rollinson (12)

I Broke

A piece of me fell
I lost my lead
And I began to dwell
On my bleak future ahead.

I lay on the desk
Not knowing my future
I forced for an exit
Past the computer
To try and discover it.

I wanted revenge
Not knowing if, when or how
So, I formed a plan
To try and find this foul
Evil little man.

My plan was simple
To end my immense suffering
I wouldn't rest until he has ended
I was the king
And he needed to accept it.

Harry Scrase (12)

Stop Looking At Me

Walk in public, eyes start to dart
Always realising that I am not in the dark
Don't look at me like that, I think
My tears nearly reaching the brink
My arms shadowing my body
Hiding all the skin
Also hiding the pain that's buried underneath
Deep in the layers of my eyes
If only I was disguised
Like one of them
As one of them
Let's see what happens if they are like me
Maybe then we'll see
If they want people to stop looking at me.

Maribel Ortiz (13)

War Horse

I see my master lying on the floor,
Waiting to see whether she will breathe once more,
Although I know her time is done,
I wish once more we had some fun,
This war is full of pain and death,
How will I live without her depth?
Her burning eyes see only the light
But now I wish I could set this right...
The burning flames of war aren't over,
So I know I will fight once more,
That is the fact that hurts me most,
The fact that I won't fight for her...

Kanchan Baishkiyar (11)

She's Fine

She always speaks,
Even about the stupidest things imaginable,
But never stops,
Talking is a coping mechanism,
It draws her thoughts away from what's really wrong,
People find her annoying and she knows,
People think they know her,
But nobody really does, not even her,

When people say,
"Hi, how are you?"
The answer is always,
"Hi, I'm fine, how are you?"
It's never the truth.

Alisha Muchova (14)

Imperfect Perfection

Day in, day out they witness my beauty,
my avant-garde design and my unparalleled complexity.
I'm a true testament to your artistic comprehension,
I'm limited to a canvas, yet its bounds don't limit my painter's intentions.

My critics are chastised,
despite my flaws not lying beyond their eyes,
because I am 'perfection without any question',
according to my praises, who all play a blind eye to my imperfections.

Dexter Warburton (15)

Forest Fire

F ire spread through the trees
O range light sprung up around me
R andom sparks flying through my leaves
E verything was moving fast
S preading wildly, burning my past
T ime was ticking on...

F ire was nearly here
I was going to die
R are was the chance of staying alive, but I had to try
E verything went dark. Death was upon me...

Eleanor Pym (11)

The Night Owl

I open my feathered wings and soar through the dark blue sky,
No other bird in sight for it is night.

I see the foxes trying to be ever so sly,
The tiny mice scurry across the long grassy fields.

The wind brushes my light feathers,
The wind is cold and fresh.

I land on a solid branch on the tops of a tree,
I find my nest, so I sit down with just my babies and me.

Layla Williams (14)

Their Eyes

Imagining life through someone else's eyes,
A journey where empathy truly lies.
Seeing the world with a different view,
Understanding perspectives old and new.

Walking in their shoes, feeling their pain,
Learning that we're not so different, just a different lane.
Through their eyes, we see the world's diverse hue,
Imagining life as if it were brand new.

Ellie Hewitt (15)

I Am Water

I am water, I flow through our Earth,
I give you hope and life, yet you don't know my worth,
You treat me as nothing and use me as a bin,
I help you to survive and I seem to never win,
You swim in my waters, but you damage my fish,
So now I shall make my final wish -
I can do amazing things, just you wait,
One day, when you decide to save me, it'll all be too late.

Harriet Eve Wingfield (14)

The Mountain's View

I feel this impending doom,
That below my precipice the world is dying.
The flame a roar, a roar while the lions are none.
A new light arises from further, climbing,
Blazing like the sun.

Since they mutated on this world,
The patristical ape,
I can do all but watch.
The only one they have, yet act like they hate,
A doomed fate we can no longer dodge.

Poppy Grace Vaghela (14)

My Unexpected Misery

I thought he was my soulmate,
I thought we were forever.
But then he acted so different,
Like we didn't belong together.
I used to phone my mum about the things that he would do,
Like coming home and saying, "You didn't leave the house, did you?"
It was like I was in prison,
Like I couldn't break free.
Just me and my unexpected misery.

Sarah Gonsalves (12)

War Zone

R unning away from ceaseless war
E verything is blood and gore
F atherless, motherless, we stand orphaned
U nder the rockets sent to destroy us
G rains of rice so precious and portioned
E ating rarely, we stay sleepless
E very night scared of death.

Alisha Marlin (13)

Not My Own

My heart
is broken.
Only slightly.

I can't
tell anyone
what happened.

It is
never to
be heard.

But it
wasn't a
man's fault.

Or the
fault of
a family...

It is
trauma, and
it's horrible.

It's not
a lovely
story to tell.

Hafsa Ahmed Bhatti (16)

This Is Me

I am under the water.
This is me, I am in the sea.
I like my free time.
In my thoughts.

I like the sea.
This is me, my boring side.
My life is not that boring.
It's full of exciting events.
I like my life.
Exciting, peaceful, enjoyable.

Hashar Ahmed (15)

Small But A Year 8

I'm small
But I give it my all
I'm weak
Though it's strength I seek
I'm confident
But sometimes unconfident
When people judge me
It's not great
But they don't know
I'm small but a Year 8.

Benson Ngembus (13)

I Am Caesar

Crossing the Rubicon with my troops' favour,
Returning to Italy, becoming Dictator,
In the past, being a Praetor,
I once felt that Alexander was greater,
Now I lie on the ground, killed by a traitor.

Callum Richard Campbell (16)

Through My Horse's Eyes At The Beach

I feel the wind
I hear my hooves
I hear my rider giggle

I touch the sand
I taste the salty air
I love splashing in the sea

I feel the fun
I feel loved!

Olivia Rose Blake (11)

YoungWriters®
Est. 1991

YOUNG WRITERS INFORMATION

We hope you have enjoyed reading this book – and that you will continue to in the coming years.

If you're a young writer who enjoys reading and creative writing, or the parent of an enthusiastic poet or story writer, do visit our website www.youngwriters.co.uk. Here you will find free competitions, workshops and games, as well as recommended reads, a poetry glossary and our blog. There's lots to keep budding writers motivated to write!

If you would like to order further copies of this book, or any of our other titles, then please give us a call or order via your online account.

Young Writers
Remus House
Coltsfoot Drive
Peterborough
PE2 9BF
(01733) 890066
info@youngwriters.co.uk

Join in the conversation!
Tips, news, giveaways and much more!

YoungWritersUK YoungWritersCW
youngwriterscw youngwriterscw